LEGACY OF LIES

THE LEGACY SERIES BOOK 2

JEN TALTY

JUPITER PRESS

This book is a work of fiction. Names, characters, places, and incidents are products of the author's imagination or used fictitiously. Any resemblance to actual events or locales or persons living or dead is entirely coincidental.

Copyright © 2021 by Jen Talty All rights reserved.

No part of this work may be used, stored, reproduced or transmitted without written permission from the publisher except for brief quotations for review purposes as permitted by law. This book is licensed for your personal enjoyment only. This book may not be re-sold or given away to other people. If you would like to share this book with another person, please purchase an additional copy for each recipient. If you're reading this book and did not purchase it, or it was not purchased for your use only, please purchase your own copy.

PRAISE FOR JEN TALTY

"*Deadly Secrets* is the best of romance and suspense in one hot read!" *NYT Bestselling Author Jennifer Probst*

"A charming setting and a steamy couple heat up the pages in a suspenseful story I couldn't put down!" *NY Times and USA today Bestselling Author Donna Grant*

"Jen Talty's books will grab your attention and pull you into a world of relatable characters, strong personalities, humor, and believable storylines. You'll laugh, you'll cry, and you'll rush to get the next book she releases!" Natalie Ann USA Today Bestselling Author

"I positively loved *In Two Weeks*, and highly recommend it. The writing is wonderful, the story is fantastic, and the characters will keep you coming back for more. I can't wait to get my hands on future installments of the NYS Troopers series." *Long and Short Reviews*

"*In Two Weeks* hooks the reader from page one. This is a fast paced story where the development of the romance grabs you emotionally and the suspense keeps you sitting on the edge of your chair. Great characters, great writing, and a believable plot that can be a warning to all of us." *Desiree Holt, USA Today Bestseller*

"*Dark Water* delivers an engaging portrait of wounded hearts as the memorable characters take you on a healing journey of love. A mysterious death brings danger and intrigue into the drama, while sultry passions brew into a believable plot that melts the reader's heart. Jen Talty pens an entertaining romance that grips the heart as the colorful and dangerous story unfolds into a chilling ending." *Night Owl Reviews*

"This is not the typical love story, nor is it the typical mystery. The characters are well rounded and interesting." *You Gotta Read Reviews*

"*Murder in Paradise Bay* is a fast-paced romantic thriller with plenty of twists and turns to keep you guessing until the end. You won't want to miss this one..." *USA Today bestselling author Janice Maynard*

LEGACY OF LIES
THE LEGACY SERIES, BOOK 2

USA Today Bestselling Author
JEN TALTY

BOOK DESCRIPTION

What if the mother you thought had died, was alive and well and living fifty miles away?

Katie Bateman's mother died years ago, or so she thought. That all changed the day a stranger came into her office asking her to find his missing wife, who looks an awful lot like her late mother. Katie, a little spooked by the resemblance, goes to her FBI friend, Jacob Donovan, whose father had been close friends with her mother and her uncle. Jacob chalks it up to someone who just looks like her mother. How could it be anyway? She was dead. Besides, Jacob is preoccupied with a case where young girls are going missing and now turning up dead.

Katie starts to uncover some inconsistencies in her new client's missing wife's case. As she digs deeper, she finds a picture of Edward's wife and it's the exact same picture, the only picture, that Katie has of her late mother.

The closer Katie gets to finding Edward's wife, her mother, the closer she comes to the final game. Edwards game.

A NOTE FROM JEN TALTY

Welcome to the second book in *The Legacy Series*, where the skeletons families thought they had well-hidden come falling out of the closet. This series does not need to be read in order!

This book is set in Lake George, New York. One of my favorite places in the entire world. I spent many summers during my youth and I enjoy visiting it, even if in my own mind. In *Legacy of Lies* I reintroduce two characters from my *New State Trooper Series*. Jared Blake from *In Two Weeks* and Stacey Sutten from *Murder in Paradise Bay* both make a brief appearance. This is also a series that does not need to be read in order. If you want to find out more about those characters, please check the *New York State Trooper Series*. The best part is *In Two Weeks* is FREE on all platforms.

Also, a few characters from the spin off *First Responders Series* make a cameo appearance. I hope you'll check them out!

For more information please visit my website at https://jentalty.com

PROLOGUE

Grace Bateman's body slammed into the passenger-side door. The near whiteout conditions made it impossible to see anything but the swirling snow outside the car. Gusting wind hammered against the speeding vehicle. The tires squealed as they failed to grip the icy roads.

"Slow down," she said. She raised her left hand and pressed it gingerly against her right shoulder. Warm liquid trickled between her fingers. She glanced at her thigh. More blood. More pain. She blinked, trying to remember what'd happened, but it was all such a blur. Her eyes burned, and tears rolled down her cheeks.

"Not an option," Thurston said.

"Turn around. I want to go back. You promised we could take her with us. You promised me you'd never separate me from my little girl."

"It's not like I wanted to do that," Thurston said as he swerved again.

She cringed, trying not to scream. "Look at me. I could bleed to death if we don't get to a hospital." Another wound at her side trickled blood down to the seat.

"I'm taking care of that. Don't worry. Why do you think I'm driving like a madman?" He placed his hand over hers and increased the pressure on one of her wounds. "This is all your brother's fault, not mine. If he'd kept his nose out of your business, we'd have all the money, and none of this would have happened. He's the one who did this to you. He's the one who shot you and stole all of your and Katie's money."

"I don't remember what happened," she whispered.

"That's because he drugged you. Had I not shown up, he would have finished you off."

"What about Katie?"

"I told you. Owen set this up to make it look like you tried to kill him. And our baby girl. If we took her, it would be an all-out witch hunt, and we'd never be safe. And neither would she. This way, they will know it was Owen, and Katie will be safe. That's all that matters."

She breathed in deeply through her nose, exhaling slowly out her mouth. She stared at Edward's strong profile. "Do you think she's going to be okay?"

"Yeah. She'll be fine." He reached out and traced the back of his index finger along Grace's cheek. "Kids are resilient. Besides, she's so beautiful and charming, she'll get adopted right away. Don't worry. She's going to grow up and make us proud. I'm sure of that."

The car skidded across the snow-covered road, nearly hitting the metal side rail meant to keep cars from tumbling into the icy waters of Lake George. Thurston gripped the steering wheel with both hands.

"It's not right that she should be without me. I'm her mother. I love her more than anyone ever could."

"I'm sorry, but we can't go back. Your brother made sure of that. And I made sure he'll pay for that mistake. He *will* pay. I promise you that."

Grace rested her head on the headrest. The snow continued racing across the night sky. She closed her eyes and pictured sweet baby Kathryn with her red hair and freckles and a smile so bright it was contagious. She was the happiest child on the planet, and all Grace could hope for was that happiness would spill over to those who ended up caring for her.

1

Katie Bateman tapped her pencil against the wood desk to the rapid beat of her partner's insanely heavy typing. Jackson was a great private investigator, one of the best, but he had some annoying habits. "You're making me nuts," she said.

He peered over his computer screen. The brown curls on the top of his head matched his hairy face. When he winked, she knew she was in trouble.

"Don't you dare," she said.

He smiled, then quickly stood, turned, and hit the little red button on the picture hanging over his head. The plastic fish sprang to life, singing *Take me to the River*.

"That's just lovely." She tossed her pencil across the room. She was going to get his wife back for buying that stupid thing. Jackson didn't even like fishing all that much. However, his son Max had taken a liking to the stupid sport. "I'm going to put my Jets cap back on if you do that again."

Jackson raised his hand and waggled a finger. "No, you're not. It's unprofessional."

"So is that thing."

He shrugged. "You'd seriously ask me to take down something that makes my little boy smile like the great state of Texas every time he comes to see his dad at the office?"

"That's not playing fair. You know how much I adore Max." She smiled. Two could play at this game. "And he loves my Jets. I really hope your next kid is a girl. She'll need an influence like me in her life."

"My wife might think otherwise." He started pounding on his keyboard again, occasionally stopping with one hand to take a sip of coffee or look at his phone, all while his other hand continued with the typing. She envied his ability to multitask and stay focused.

She also tried not to be jealous of his family life. And not just Shannon and his son. But also, his parents and siblings. Jackson had everything. All she had was a murderous uncle. For years, she hadn't felt sorry for herself. She always told herself that life was what she made of it, and she'd done quite well. But the decision to move into the family home had stirred so many emotions, her strong, confident demeanor had taken a hit.

Of course, having Jacob hanging around all the time didn't help either.

She fingered the pendant dangling from her neck and leaned back in her chair. The cool silver metal glided across her fingers, soothing her ragged nerves. Thankfully, the singing fish had stopped, and the only noise was the rhythmic beat of Jackson's fingers. As much as the sound sometimes distracted her, it also had a calming effect. "Any news on the Williams' case?"

He paused in his typing for a moment. "It seems to have run cold."

"That's not good." Katie hadn't known the Williams girl well, but she did know the girl's parents and had promised she'd do what she could. "I've got a bad feeling about this one."

"Yeah, so do I," Jackson said. "Your uncle is on the move."

"Where to?" She released the necklace and grabbed the mouse on her desk, giving it a quick jiggle to awaken her computer. "I have no email messages from Horace."

"He sent me a text." Jackson lifted his phone and waved it in her direction. "Uncle O is at the drug store down the street from his apartment. So far, he hasn't done anything suspicious. Yet."

"Everything he does is suspicious. Eventually, he is going to crack and give me what I want."

Jackson sat up taller and peered over his computer screen. "He hasn't cracked in twenty-seven years."

"He moved back here for one reason and one reason only. The money is here. And the money is going to lead me to my mother." It still amazed her that they'd convicted her uncle for murder without a body. That was rare, but her mother wouldn't just up and abandon her only child. That didn't make sense.

"You need to face facts." Jackson raised a brow. "You've been having your uncle tailed for the last two years, and nothing. Not one single lead. What makes you think now will be any different?"

"You're spending too much time with Jacob."

"Maybe you're not spending *enough* time with Jacob. I know deep down you really want to forgive him and move—"

"Let's not go there," she said before Jackson could start playing matchmaker again. Jackson leaned back in his chair and stared at her from across the office. "You're too hard on Jacob."

Thankfully, Katie heard footsteps climbing the stairs of the old office building. The last thing she wanted to do was get into a detailed discussion about one Agent Jacob Donovan. No matter how adorable, kind, and sweet the man could be, he'd broken her heart, and she wasn't about to forget with who. "Sounds like our potential client is here." She curled the strands of her long, red hair, counting the steps of the approaching stranger. You could tell a lot about a man by his walk. This guy took his time. His steps were evenly spaced. It was a hesitant gait, indicating that he was a thinker. Every once in a while, a client would show up, get halfway up the stairs, then turn around and bolt.

This man was now a third of the way, a good indication that he wasn't suffering from a case of cold feet.

Jackson stood and moved across the room. He had this idea that greeting people at the door before they even had to knock, showed the possible client that Bateman and Associates cared about their situation. Katie thought it showed desperation. But, so far, it seemed to be working for them, and the reality was, they needed the money.

"Mr. Howell?" Jackson asked.

"Yes. You must be Jackson," a deep voice replied.

Katie inched her way across the room. The richness of the man's voice intrigued her. He spoke slowly and pronounced each syllable as if he were an English scholar. Her brief search into Edward's background had netted very little.

"This is my partner, Katie Bateman." Jackson turned, taking a small step back, allowing Edward into the office.

Edward carried an old-fashioned leather briefcase in his left hand. The kind that had one of those combination locks. He had dark hair with matching intense brown eyes. He didn't smile but rather nodded slightly as he approached her with an extended hand. He clasped his fingers firmly around hers and shook once. His skin was soft and warm but with a few calluses.

His stats indicated that he was sixty-three. He had deep lines etched in his face, but they didn't make him look old—rather well-lived. She offered him a seat near the window. A momentary awkward silence filled the air as Jackson took his seat in his office chair, and she rolled hers across the room to in front of Jackson's desk.

"I'm sorry about the circumstances that led you to our office," Katie began. "I want to be upfront with you."

Edward nodded, so she continued.

"It has been our experience in cases like this that our clients are not happy with the outcome," she said.

"I know what you are thinking," Edward said. "That my wife ran off with some younger man or something. But that isn't the case."

"All right." Katie had learned to let her clients believe whatever they wanted in the beginning. The truth would come out sooner or later, and it wasn't her job to make them believe, just find the answer that they really didn't want to know deep down, but needed to find out to be able to move forward in their lives. "Why did she leave?"

Edward tilted his head and looked to his upper right. "I have always been supportive of my wife's... well, let's call them issues." He adjusted his pants then crossed his legs. "She never explained them all, but I knew she had a dark past."

"What do you mean by a dark past?" Jackson asked.

"She had a troubled childhood." Edward shifted in his seat and looked out the window. "She said it was too painful to talk about, even with the man she loved." He pressed a finger against his lips. "She went to a therapist once a week, no matter where we lived. I never questioned. She said it helped her to cope. The very few times she did not go, I could see the change in her, so I encouraged it. I love her. I just want her to be happy."

"Did you report your wife missing?" Katie asked. She took mental notes about his body language and the way he searched for just the right word.

Edward let out a long breath as he glanced between her and Jackson. "No."

Katie leaned forward, resting her hands on her thighs. "Why not?"

"We all have a legacy of lies we don't wish to pass on or have the things we love tainted by it. We hide it in the closet or bury it in the sand. But, inevitably, our secrets come spilling out."

Katie wondered what secrets Edward had hidden deep. Because if what he said was true, she was sure he had a few. "So, she left you because she found out you lied to her, is that correct?"

"No," Edward said with a defiant tone as if she'd insulted him. "She didn't leave me. She needed space. I gave her that. But it's been weeks, and I'm worried."

"I understand," Jackson said. "Please, tell us what you lied about."

"You have to understand that I did this to protect my wife." Edward ran his forefinger and thumb across his square chin.

This ought to be interesting.

"I made up a past that I thought would impress her. I was young and totally infatuated with MaryAnn—that's my wife's name. It was obvious to me that she came from high society and expected to live a certain lifestyle. I had money, but…" He paused, shifting his gaze up and to the right again. "I came by my money in a way that she would not have approved of."

"And how *did* you come into your money?" Jackson asked.

"I gambled. I still gamble, but not like I used to. I don't do high-stake tables anymore, but I didn't tell her about any of it, and that upset her."

"That's a tough way to make money," Katie said.

Jackson had his pen out, and his hand moved quickly across the legal pad. Katie wanted to know what he was scribbling. He could read people better than anyone she'd ever met, and he was almost always spot-on.

"Well, I've invested well, and now my gambling is a fun game with friends. But I still kept it from her."

"What makes you think she came here?" Katie asked.

"From what little she told me about the life she left behind, I know she has family here."

Jackson put his pencil down and leaned back in his

chair. "If she had a troubled childhood, why would she come back to a family she may have run from?"

"She spoke fondly of the area. Especially Lake George." He raised his hand to his face and rubbed his eyes. "I also got the impression there might have been a person or two she missed. I don't know if they were family members or friends, but I know it was hard for her to break from her past, even if it was horrific."

"So why are you worried, if you think she's with an old friend?" Katie kept her gaze on Edward's face. She noticed that he rarely blinked. And that when he searched for the right words, his eyes widened as if to let the information he searched for appear in his mind.

Edward wore designer clothing, and his shoes were freshly polished. He didn't appear to be a gambler or someone who got off on risk-taking. His demeanor was more that of a well-educated man with a flair for self-importance. She saw him as either a really good con artist, or a solid citizen.

"MaryAnn left a brief voice message shortly after she left. She told me she would be home in a week. That we'd talk then."

"You think something bad happened?" Jackson asked.

"I have no idea. But I have a bad feeling, which is why I contacted you."

"What is your wife's maiden name?" Jackson asked.

"Our marriage license states Grant. MaryAnn Grant." Edward reached for his briefcase, placing it on his lap as he clicked open the latches. "But she was honest in telling me that wasn't her given name. She had it changed when she left her family behind. She didn't want them ever finding her. I have no idea what her real name is." He pulled out a manila envelope.

"Was the name change legal?" Katie knew in her gut that Edward was lying or at least lying by omission about something. Most clients usually did. No reason for him to be any different. But the question was always…why? Who was he protecting? His wife? Or himself?

Edward swiped at his eyes again. There were no tears, but Katie could see the strong emotion behind the tough exterior. "I don't know. And until now, I've never cared. I should have come clean about my past long ago. There was absolutely no good reason for the deception, especially after nearly twenty-seven years of marriage." He handed Katie the envelope. "I know she had a reason to lie. No one leaves a family behind without good reason, and I could see the pain in her eyes every time I brought it up, which is why I didn't do that very often."

Edward reached back into his briefcase and pulled out a letter-sized envelope. "I brought cash in the amount you stated would be your retainer and then doubled it for expenses or whatever else you might bill me for. I don't want to go and interview a bunch of private investigators. I did my homework and have decided that the two of you are the best. I'm willing to pay for it."

Katie riffled through the papers that she had pulled out of the envelope while Jackson, as politely as possible, looked at the cash inside the other envelope. His right brow rose slightly. "Do you plan on staying in the area?"

"For a few days." Edward snapped his briefcase closed and stood. "Vegas is an interesting place. Most people say it is the city where people go to die. In my wife's case, when she left home, she was wandering about aimlessly, and Sin City seemed like a place she could stay lost in. However, she was also reborn in that city when she took on my name."

"Do you have any other information that might help us?" Katie asked, looking at the Vegas marriage license.

"I wish I did. All I want is the opportunity to explain everything to MaryAnn. I love her, more than any words can express."

"This isn't a lot to go on." Katie held up the few papers he had given her.

"Everything I know about her past, you have in your hands."

Katie stood and moved over to Jackson's desk where she could spread out everything that Edward had given her. She moved them around until she uncovered the pictures. Her heart skipped a beat. She traced her finger across the image of an aging, blonde woman, her finger stopping under the woman's eyes.

Her face had had a little too much plastic surgery. Her skin over-bronzed from a combination of too much sun and makeup. She looked older than sixty. She was skinny, and her smile was forced. She certainly didn't look like a happy woman.

"When I first walked into this office and saw you, I was stunned by how much your eyes remind me of my wife's." Tears appeared in Edward's orbs. "We couldn't have a child. That was something that always hurt my wife."

Katie's heart pounded. "I'm sorry," was all she could manage.

"Do you have any photos of her when she was younger?" Jackson asked.

"Yes," Edward said. "But I assumed you'd want recent shots."

"Pictures from when you first met would be helpful," Jackson said. "Or even any you might have from when she was in high school. That might help us find her real name and where she might have gone."

"All right. I have some in my hotel. I will bring them over to you…say tomorrow?"

"How about if Jackson picks them up tonight?" Katie continued to stare at the image of the woman with the familiar eyes.

"That would be fine." Edward jotted down his hotel information. "I appreciate you taking my business."

"We will do our best to find your wife." Katie walked him to the door, shook his hand, and watched him walk down the stairs. His steps followed the same pattern out the door as they had when he first entered the building. "His wife's eyes look just like my mother's." Katie turned. Her eyes burned as she fought tears. "If you put red hair on that woman, I bet she'd look just like my mom...just like me."

"They say everyone has a twin." Jackson gathered up all the papers and shoved them into the envelope.

"It's creepy. Not to mention, they have been married for twenty-seven years."

"I can't believe I'm going to say this, but it's just an odd coincidence," Jackson said.

Katie went to her desk, snagged her Jets cap, pulled her ponytail through the back hole, and tugged on the visor until the cap was firmly in place. "As sure as I am that I'm going to find that man's wife, I'm going to make my uncle tell me where he disposed of my mother's body, and what the hell he did with all my family's money." Her cell phone buzzed. She snagged it off the desk and read the text. "Shit, my house was just broken into." She glanced at Jackson. "How much do you want to bet it was Owen?"

*A*gent Jacob Donovan sat in his chair staring at a half-dozen photographs of dead girls whose killers had never been brought to justice. All he needed was a solid connection, linking them to a recent case, preferably a national case, and he'd get the green light.

He secured his spot in the middle so he'd have a three-hundred-and-sixty-degree-angle overview. What he really wanted to do was move his and his partner's desks out into the hallway to make more room. There was a new stack of papers on the corner that a buddy of his with the Violent Crimes Unit had been kind enough to fax over. Missing redheaded girls between the ages of sixteen and twenty-five, spanning the last ten years. The Behavioral Science Unit, was tasked with trying to profile one or more of these girls to the Williams girl, but that didn't mean Jacob couldn't take it upon himself to give his colleagues down in DC a helping hand.

Of course, his boss might not appreciate the effort.

Jacob ran a hand across the stubble on his face as he tried to see the patterns that weren't obvious but he knew to be right under his nose. It was there. He just had to find it. His partner interrupted his thought process. "Well, if it isn't my partner in crime. The boy genius."

"Why the hell do you call me that?" Cameron Thatcher asked with a slight edge to his voice.

"Because it's true," Jacob said. "You're a fucking genius, and you're a goddamned boy."

"I'm a grown-ass adult."

Jacob laughed. "But you didn't deny being brilliant."

"On that, I will plead the fifth."

"Aren't you humble?"

"How am I supposed to get to my desk?" Cameron might be a newbie to the FBI, but his instincts had proven razor-sharp on the last case. Everyone in the office had chalked it up to a little bit of luck on a case that had been about to crack anyway. Jacob knew differently. Cameron's ability to read people—both dead and alive—was something that couldn't be taught. He was a natural profiler, and Jacob tried not to be jealous.

"For now, you don't," Jacob said. "You stand there and look at all of this." He loosened his tie and unbuttoned the top button of his shirt. "Then you sit on the floor and you look some more." Jacob picked up a stack of printouts from his desk and began matching the pictures of the girls when they'd been alive to the crime scene photos.

"All right." Cameron shoved his hands into his pockets and started staring at the pictures. Jacob watched him for a few minutes, curious to see if he could figure out how the kid's mind worked. The boy wonder was a damn fucking genius. "What am I looking at?"

"Six dead girls."

"I can see that," Cameron said. "What's the connection?"

"All disappeared. All found murdered in the Adirondacks over the last twenty-seven years. All have red hair. And that's all I've got."

Cameron was barely a man at twenty-three. He had intense dark brown eyes, which always made him look serious, even when cracking a joke. He parted his short, dark hair on the side, which made him look somewhat nerdy, but that didn't seem to detract the girls' attention or stop them from swarming him during happy hour.

Jacob had pegged him as the quiet, determined type in school. Not a loner or anything. More of a kid with goals where everything else was merely a distraction. Jacob used to be that driven back when he first started —before everything got all fucked up.

"You're trying to connect these to *The Doe Hunter*," Cameron said.

"The connection is there. We just have to find it," Jacob said. "The thing is, there are subtle differences, and the majority of his kills happened on the west coast, not here. But what if he got his start here and has now decided to revisit his humble beginnings for some reason?"

"You think this missing Williams girl could be another victim, and you believe tying her to these other women will give us a lead?"

"I'm not looking for a lead. I'm just looking to prove

it's him. Right now, I'm focusing on cold cases that might have been overlooked in years past. Most of these are cases our team has never seen. If we can make a real connection, we can go on an all-out manhunt."

"There are more than twenty-seven years between one of these cases and the Williams girl."

"We could easily have one of the biggest monsters of the century." Jacob let out a long breath. Not to mention, the biggest case of his career. Although, he couldn't help but think about what it would be like to prosecute a bastard like this.

"Okay," Cameron said. "The three found at the river's edge don't match the current profile of *The Doe Hunter*."

Jacob turned his chair until he found each of those cases and picked them off the floor. "Why don't you think they match?"

"*The Doe Hunter* only uses weapons associated with big game hunting. And not just any hunting—sport hunting. Those girls were shot with small-caliber handguns."

"All right, but we have to look at how he may have perfected his crime over the course of many years. These could have been his first kills." Jacob continued looking at the pictures on the floor.

"Yes, but if the hunt is part of this man's psyche, he wouldn't have used a handgun, even early in his career. A large knife or even a shotgun meant more for small game perhaps, but not a handgun." Cameron took a step to the right and pointed at the desk. "One thing I noticed was that the girls who have been successfully linked to *The Doe Hunter* were all under the age of twenty-three."

"All right." Jacob reached down and plucked two from the floor. "What are you thinking?"

"I'm not sure yet," Cameron said. "What about their victimology? Do we have those reports?"

"I've asked. Everything any law enforcement agency had that referenced these particular cases is right here in this room."

"For most of them, the family stated that they had wild aspirations of being a star or were chasing some dream. Where is the case file on Veronica Hemming?"

"Um…it's around here somewhere." Jacob pushed around a few of the case files until he found it. "She was ruled out because her cause of death was dehydration, though she *had* been stabbed with a hunting knife."

"The thing is, her body wasn't staged like all the other victims. But she was found in the middle of the Dix Range, naked, and it appeared she was trying to hide in the bushes. She wasn't dead when they found her, but she died just hours after she got to the hospital. What if she was his first victim? Or one of his firsts?" Cameron said. "I don't think there is any case even close to *The Doe Hunter* before that one."

"You really do have a photographic memory, don't you?"

Cameron shrugged. "My mother used to tell me I was a walking font of useless information."

"Definitely not useless."

"Trust me. There is some useless information between these ears." Cameron sat down on the floor and crossed his legs. "You have some interesting ways of analyzing information."

"Tricking the brain."

"It's confusing my mind."

"That sort of makes me happy," Jacob said.

"I'm not sure the Williams girl fits the victimology. According to her family, she had no desire to be an actress or model."

"She was studying film. She still had dreams of going to Hollywood, but it was as a film producer. She was quite ambitious. Her parents said she would have done just about anything to achieve her goals."

"But if our profile is right, this guy is looking for someone who is easily manipulated and almost desperate to make it to the big leagues. The interview with Cassidy's parents doesn't portray her that way. She was more meticulous and wanted to do it on the merits of her work."

"She was a very intelligent young girl, but that doesn't mean she didn't have a weakness that our killer exposed," Jacob said. "There are four things that all of these girls have in common. They have red hair. They are physically fit. They wanted to have a career in the entertainment business and are believed to have known the killer for at least a short period of time. I don't think family relations play that big of a role in how the killer targets his victims. What we need to focus on now is who was in these girls' lives during the last few weeks before they went missing." Jacob started collecting the pictures and placing them back in the appropriate file. It was getting late, and he still had to stop by his parents'. That wasn't going to be a pleasant visit.

"I heard the Williamses hired a local PI."

"Yeah. Katie Bateman. She's a friend of mine. Good investigator. She hooked them up with someone she knows in Los Angeles."

Cameron stood and placed all the pictures on the desk before sitting down in his chair. "No offense, but in my experience, PIs are useless and generally don't feed us good intel."

"Because you have a ton of experience," Jacob said with a roll of his eyes. He liked Cameron. A lot. But this kind of comment grated on his last nerve. "And Katie's not useless. She's got more smarts than half the people in this office."

"PIs are either burnt-out cops or cop wannabes. I can't understand why you value them so much."

Jacob was about to set the kid straight when the receptionist stuck her head into the office. "You should check your cell. Jackson's been trying to get ahold of you. The Bateman place was broken into." Cindy had been the receptionist for the local FBI office for ten years. You needed information; she was your girl. She knew more than the special agent in charge.

"Did Jackson say if the locals had a suspect?" Jacob asked. The sucky part about working in Albany and living in Lake George was the fucking hour-long commute. But that was his choice, all because he was still hung up on his ex-girlfriend.

"Nope. But Jackson says Owen Bateman has an airtight alibi," Cindy said. "And for the record, the local at the scene is—"

"Your boyfriend." As if Jacob expected anything different.

"It doesn't look too bad, but Katie's pissed and hell-bent on proving that it was her uncle, Owen."

"I'm sure she is. And I'm it was," Jacob said. He checked the time. "What do we have left to finish up today?"

"Nothing," Cameron said. "Tell me more about this Owen Bateman guy."

"Not much to tell." Jacob did his best to keep his frustration in check. "He did twenty-five years and my dad was his attorney." It had been a long time since anyone had brought up any of this, but when Owen was released from prison two years ago, the shit hit the fan. "Why do you want to know?"

"I'm curious."

"Curiosity killed the cat."

"I'm not implying anything," Cameron said. His tone was even as always. The man would be great at poker. His face never gave anything away except for the fact that he was always thinking. About what? Well, that was up for grabs at any given moment, but Jacob was sure it was likely about work or work-related things. "The case is all over the news, and I thought it would be better to ask you instead of going to the archives."

Jacob put the files in his desk, then took his keys from the top drawer. "If you go through the archives, let me know what you find."

"Seriously?"

"Yeah, seriously. They won't let me near the case."

"You've never asked anyone to look for you?"

Jacob smiled. "No comment. And I'm not asking."

"Enough said."

"And they all said you were a strictly by-the-books kind of guy." Jacob was pleasantly surprised that Cameron would even consider looking through the files. Only one other person had ever done so, but they'd gotten cold feet about giving Jacob whatever intel was there—which only meant bad news.

"So it would appear," Cameron said, and for the first time in the two weeks Jacob had been working with him, he smiled. "But you really shouldn't judge a book by its cover."

"I'll remember that."

2

Katie stood in the middle of the back porch of the Bateman family estate, clutching the pillow from the recliner and wishing it was her uncle's neck. The dark waters of Lake George glistened under the white moon in the distance. "Unbelievable." She tossed the pillow to the sofa, then bent over and picked up the picture of her mother off the floor. Broken glass distorted the beautiful image, but thankfully, the photograph was intact. She glanced around at the rest of the vandalized sunroom. The chairs had been overturned. A book tossed carelessly to the floor. Papers scattered. Door busted in. It reminded her of the night long ago that still gave her nightmares. In the dreams, she could only see bits and pieces of reality that collided with the strangeness of the subconscious and the stories she'd read in the papers. She'd been too young to remember. There was only one other living person who knew the truth, and he wasn't talking.

"This is the only thing that is actually broken," she said, more to herself than to Officer Crane, who was fiddling with the back door. "And nothing is missing."

"What about in the rest of the house?"

"From what I can tell, everything is in order. Either Owen's playing with me, or something spooked him, and he took off before he got whatever he was looking for."

"You know damn well Owen didn't do this," Crane said.

"Then he hired someone."

Crane tilted his head. "It could have been a bunch of teenagers." A childhood memory of Crane running through the backyard as she chased him because he was a robber and she was the cop flashed in front of her. A smile tugged at her lips.

"Besides, you can account for every move your uncle has made from the second he decided to come back here."

"Not every second," she said. "He's a slippery bastard."

Crane nodded, refocusing on trying to find a way to lock the door, as she went back to staring at the picture of her late mother.

Crane opened and closed the door a few times and checked the latch. "This needs to be replaced. I can't get it to lock. I can come back after my shift is over with a new door from my dad's shop if you'd like. No problem."

"Thanks. But I've actually got a new door with a deadbolt sitting in the garage. I'm sure I can handle it." She tugged at a piece of the glass, slipping the image from the frame. Her mother's eyes were a light blue, and in this picture, full of life and promise.

She had so few memories of her mom. What she did have, came in home movies, pictures, and stories. She cherished every single one—even those that didn't paint the rosy picture Katie wanted to remember her mother by. But Katie was a realist, and knowing the truth helped her understand her mother's tortured soul.

"Even though there will be a car in the neighborhood, I recommend doing it now," Crane said. He closed the door and then pulled a chair over, leaning it against the door and hooking it under the handle. "If you don't mind me asking, what is up with you and Jacob?"

"Nothing," Katie said. "We've just come to an understanding." She shifted to the side, allowing Crane to step ahead of her. She followed him through the family room, still holding the picture. "He didn't think I should rattle around in this big, old house by myself, especially when my uncle returned. And I had to agree."

"That was a smart move, but I'm surprised he agreed to move in with you."

She turned and glared. "You should be more surprised that I let him."

"I'm only shocked that the two of you aren't an item."

Katie opted to change the subject. "Has Cindy accepted the marriage proposal yet?"

"I gave her the ring and stopped asking. Told her when she was ready, just to put it on."

"You're a good man," Katie said.

"So I'm told."

She set the picture on the table by the front door. She'd find a new frame soon enough. "Thanks for coming," she said.

"I'll be in the neighborhood until midnight. You've got my cell number if you need me."

"Why don't you go out the garage?" She walked through the kitchen into the great room, which led to the back mudroom. She opened the door and hit the garage door opener. A misty rain filtered through the glow of the lights. A dense grey cloud loomed over the back of the Bateman estate, waiting to open its floodgates. She watched Crane stroll to his patrol car. He examined the yard, making one last check for the menacing predator.

"Watch your back," Crane said. He pointed to the large wrought-iron gate that blocked the long driveway from the street. "Shut this."

"It doesn't work. It's on the long list of things to get

fixed." Her throat tightened. "Besides, I know where Owen is hiding."

"This wasn't the work of your uncle, and you know that. Shut the gate."

Quickly, she hit the button. The motor to the garage door hummed to life. She closed the house door and clicked the lock in place. She turned and walked right into Jackson. "Shit. Where the fuck did you come from?"

"The chair on the front door doesn't make for a lock," Jackson said.

She reached up and touched his freshly shaven face. "Did you shave as soon as you got home?"

"Shannon absolutely hated it. Told me not only no kisses but that I'd be sleeping on the sofa."

Katie laughed. "I love your wife."

Jackson laughed. "You've grown on her."

"Why did you come back?"

"It's pizza night," Jackson said. "It won't be ready for another twenty minutes."

"Did you go get the pictures from Edward?"

"He called me and said he'd send them over to the office in the morning."

"I find that fishy, don't you?" She padded to the kitchen, needing a nice tall shot of whiskey. The day had gone from strange to downright bad. She pulled down a glass and waved it in front of Jackson.

He shook his head. "I'll wait to pass judgement. If

they don't show up at the office by noon, then we'll know something isn't right in Kansas."

"That's the dumbest saying I've ever heard." She tossed back a double shot. The burn felt so good in the back of her throat. "And we need to fire your buddy, Horace. Obviously, he's not tracking my uncle very well."

"You have to accept the fact that Owen didn't do this."

"You sound like Crane."

"Well, Crane's a smart guy. But I wouldn't put it past your uncle to hire someone. So, until we figure it out, we'll take extra precautions. Clear?" He took her by the forearm. "Now, why don't I help you install that front door?"

"I can do it myself, and you have some food to get."

"But I know you. If we don't do it now, it will never get done."

She laughed, but only because he was right. She slapped the button on the rickety old garage as it lifted to life once again. That was going to break one of these days, too. Everything in this rundown place was on its last legs. But she couldn't sell the damn thing because of the lean on it thanks to her uncle and all the money he stole. Until they found that, this place was in limbo.

The sound of a car rumbled in the night. "Crane's patrol car sounds like it needs to be put out of its misery."

Katie turned and stepped into the garage. "That's

not Crane. It's Jacob. The muffler must have finally fallen off." She shook her head. "The man can afford a new vehicle. I don't understand why he won't let go of that hunk of junk."

"You know, you and he are a lot alike in that way."

"I'm nothing like Jacob." Absently, she brought her hand to the specially designed locket dangling from her neck. She ran her fingers across the engraved lettering; D-A-U-G-H-T-E-R.

"Then why is he living here?"

Truth be told, she had no idea. Jacob had given her some song and dance about wanting to be closer to his folks and considering buying a place on the lake, but he hadn't found anything yet—something she didn't understand. He worked an hour away. He woke up every day at five-thirty, was out the door by six, and often didn't get home until eight. Not that she kept any better hours.

She made her way through the large family room, which was still in need of some serious renovation. She'd have the money soon enough. A greedy man never changed his ways, no matter how long they'd spent in prison. Owen would lead her to both her mother's body and the stolen money. He had to.

When she entered the kitchen, she grabbed the remote and clicked on the news. The weatherman predicted chilly temperatures and rain. She set the remote aside and opened her backpack, which she had left on the kitchen table. She pulled out some files and rested them against the other stack of papers she'd set there earlier. She sighed. Even with all her experience and training, she couldn't find one dead body and a few million missing dollars.

She decided it was better to have some hot chocolate than another double shot—though that might not be out of the question later. She filled the kettle with water and lit the stove. Hot chocolate had a soothing effect on her, and this evening certainly called for it.

The newscaster recapped the latest national headlines. Katie paused for a moment when they mentioned that a local college student, Cassidy Williams, had gone missing when she and a few of her friends had taken a trip to LA for a film workshop. She had helped the Williamses find a good PI when the locals hadn't been willing to do much after they had filed the missing person's report. Now, it seemed the FBI and Special Agent Donovan were on the case, trying to connect it to other murders.

Another good reason to have Jacob around.

A familiar female voice boomed through the television. Hannah Madison, up-and-coming reporter, who would step on her own mother if it meant a story and a possible transfer to a bigger, better station.

"It has been twenty-seven years since the murder of socialite Grace Bateman, which left a four-year old Katie without a mother or an uncle," Hannah said, standing in front of Katie's mansion. *"The mystery of Grace's death still looms over this city. And the man who was convicted of her*

murder was released from prison two years ago and recently moved back to the Lake George area, causing quite a stir among the residents."

Katie heard footsteps approaching the kitchen, and her pulse rose.

"Honey, I'm home," Jacob called in that all-too-sexy voice.

She turned up the volume.

Jackson arched a brow.

"All eyes are on Owen Bateman. His sister's body has never been found, and millions of dollars are still missing."

"Why do you insist on watching this station when I'm not around?" Jacob stretched out his arm and shook Jackson's hand.

"You used to like her." Katie kept her eyes glued to the television. "Besides, Hannah might actually have something of interest to say."

"Not possible," Jacob said under his breath as he tossed his backpack on the counter. He snagged a mug and a packet of hot chocolate. "She's a scum-sucking bottom-feeder who would toss her own mother under the bus."

"Hey, she's your girlfriend," Katie fired back.

"She's barely my ex-girlfriend, and I'd prefer to forget that time in my life." Jacob took the remote and turned off the television. He stood at the end of the table. He pushed back his sport coat when he placed his hands on his hips. "How are you holding up?" Jacob stood tall at about six-one. He was a solid mass of muscle but not bulky. He looked as good in a pair of old college sweatpants as he did in a suit. Handsome was too mild of a word. Gorgeous didn't cut it, either. Breathtaking was the only proper way to describe his good looks, and he stole her breath every time he came within a five-mile radius.

"I'm fine," she said.

Today, Jacob sported perfectly pressed black slacks with a light blue shirt, unbuttoned at the top. His wavy, brown hair touched the back of his collar. The FBI must have lowered their regulation haircut standards.

"The police have questioned your uncle," Jacob said.

"So we heard," Jackson acknowledged.

"Airtight alibi." Jacob pulled back the chair and sat. "They've got nothing to tie him to the break-in." Jacob started thumbing through the papers on the table. "Then again, you already knew that."

"Leave those alone, please," Katie said.

"If you want to send your uncle back to prison, you've got to stop working against the system." Jacob kept his hands on the stack of papers, and his ice-blue eyes locked with hers. "And you've got to stop fighting me every step of the way."

"I've tried to tell her that," Jackson said.

"I really don't care about your system. I only want to find my mother's body and pay proper respect."

"And I want to help," Jacob said.

Tears welled in her eyes. Thankfully, the kettle started to whistle, giving her a much-needed moment to collect herself. She poured the hot water into both her and Jacob's mug, plunking a good handful of marshmallows on top. "Do you want some, Jackson?"

"No. I really need to get going. But that front door needs to be fixed."

"I'll take care of it. You go." Jacob waved his hand.

"Don't you have some big meeting with your dad?" Katie asked.

"I do. But he's five minutes away. He knows I'm here."

Jackson gave her a hug before heading toward the garage. A long silence filled the kitchen as she stirred her chocolate, watching the marshmallows melt in the dark liquid.

"I'm trying to help you," Jacob said.

His whisper startled her, and she jumped, almost spilling the hot cocoa.

"We've can use the law to our advantage," he said.

"We are not in this together." She stirred the contents of her mug so vigorously, a marshmallow flipped out onto the table. She scooped it up and put it into her mouth. "Your precious law fucked up when they set a murderer free." Katie waved the spoon toward Jacob. "And your father defended that bastard. Not to mention, your dear old dad cheated on his wife with my mother."

Jacob let out a long breath. "Let the past go."

She couldn't do that. And he, of all people, should understand. But he didn't, and she couldn't change him. "Is that a ploy for me to forgive you? Because that will never happen." She hadn't meant the words to sound so harsh, but she'd had all the emotional upheaval she could handle for one night.

"No. I've learned you're going to stay angry at me for the rest of my life. But that doesn't change the fact that, right now, our worlds have collided." He stared at her, and she knew that look. He had something to say that would bother her. "What's going on?" she asked.

"Your uncle got a job at the Glens Falls Hospital."

"Seriously?" She arched a brow. "I wondered why he'd gone there a couple of times. What's he doing?"

"Administration," Jacob said. "A far cry from the respected shrink he used to be." Jacob took a big gulp of his hot chocolate and leaned against the counter. "I'll go change my clothes. I want to fix that door before I go see my folks."

"How is your mom?"

"You always ask about her, never my dad."

She laughed. "Do I really need to respond to that?"

Jacob ran a hand through his hair. "They are both fine. I'm going to go fix that door. You can help. Or not. Up to you."

She took her mug and made her way to the sliding glass doors. She stepped outside. A cool breeze rolled in off the lake. The Bateman family estate stood at the end of Rockhurst Road. She'd heard stories of when the rundown home was the envy of every boater passing by with its unique, sleek modern style, vast yard, and panoramic views of the beautiful lake nestled in the Adirondacks.

She knew she was being hard on Jacob. Even harder on his father. They had both done so much for her over the years. But she just couldn't get past the fact that Raif Donovan, Attorney at Law, had defended the man who'd murdered his mistress.

Jacob slipped a T-shirt over his head and tucked it into his jeans, securing them with a dark belt. He'd made a few mistakes over the years, but none so bad as the day he'd let Katie walk out of his life.

Or worse, the day he'd let Hannah in.

And Katie would never let him forget the latter.

He found his cell on the top of the dresser and texted his father, letting him know that he'd be a few minutes late. His old man could wait. The door could not. He should have fixed the damn thing weeks ago, but ever since the Williams girl had gone missing, his world had been turned upside down—and not just with work.

With Katie. Somehow, he had to make things right.

He jogged down the steps.

Another thing that needed fixing. Of course, she'd probably go bankrupt just trying to maintain the place, and she wouldn't take any money from him. Not even rent. And then there were all the stories that loomed over the Bateman family estate. Rumors of it being haunted. Or that her mother's body was buried somewhere on the premises. It didn't help that Grace's body had never been found. Or that Owen had decided to move back to the area. What upset Jacob more was that his father didn't seem to be bothered by the development.

Owen Bateman had destroyed so many lives, and he was still doing it.

Well, Jacob would put an end to it. He had to. For Katie's sake.

As he made his way toward the garage for the door and some tools, he saw Katie standing on the wraparound deck, facing Sandy Bay. It had been hard for her when her uncle was released from prison. Even harder when he'd moved to Lake George.

All Jacob wanted was to wrap his arms around her and tell her that it would be okay. He wanted to protect her from the big, bad wolf. But Katie had built a wall around herself that no one could break down. She'd always been slightly withdrawn, even when they were younger, but she'd kept him close for a long time.

He wanted to go back to the way things used to be.

She glanced over her shoulder and nodded as she turned, heading in his direction.

She'd decided to help. He wasn't sure if that was a good thing, or a bad idea. If they spent too much time together, they often fought.

And about stupid shit.

Or the past.

Both equally painful.

She stood at the entryway and snagged the toolkit. "Can you handle carrying the door yourself?"

"I think I can manage." Living with Katie had proven interesting. At first, they'd barely spoken, keeping a safe distance so they didn't kill each other. But when the Williams girl went missing, things changed.

Half the things he discussed with her, he shouldn't. But he didn't care. Katie was about the smartest girl he'd ever met, and her investigative skills were spot-on. Hell, she made him wonder if he'd taken a wrong turn in his career choice half the time.

He leaned the door against the wall and watched Katie as she used a small power tool to take the hinges off the old door. "You're kind of sexy when you do that."

"And you're still an asshole."

He laughed as he grabbed hold of the broken wood, helping her set it aside. "You've called me worse."

She glanced up. "Why do you keep doing that?"

"Doing what?" He took a screwdriver and undid the old hardware, then started working on putting in the new, ensuring it lined up perfectly.

"It's like you want to talk about what happened and start a fight."

"I definitely don't want to argue, but I do want to

have a conversation—something you've never really given me the opportunity to do."

She rolled her eyes, handing him a few screws and the power tool. "There's nothing to say. Other than I'm working on being friends." She actually smiled.

Genuinely.

Well, it was a start.

For the next fifteen minutes, they worked in tandem until the door was not only on the hinges but also opening and closing properly. He had to admit, friendship sounded nice, and it was something he could live with.

For now.

But he wanted more.

"What do you want for a PIN number on the lock?" he asked.

"Same as everything else."

He arched a brow. "Our birth dates?"

She shrugged. "I'm a creature of habit."

"Twenty-two, eighteen it is." His heart sped up. He tried not to take that as any kind of sign. He'd gotten his hopes up the day he'd moved in, but they were quickly shut down when he tried to kiss her, and she wasn't overeager to participate. "Are you going to be okay for a little while? I need to stop by my folks' for a bit."

"Yeah. Jackson and I got a new case that I need to do some research on. I'll just take that up to my room."

"What kind of case?"

"Missing person."

"Anything I can help with?" Jacob asked. One of these days, he would get caught using his resources as a federal agent to help Katie with some of her cases. But when he could, he was more than willing to help.

Within reason.

"My client says he never reported her missing. He says she's from the area, but that her maiden name is fake. I don't have any pictures from her past. Just one that eerily reminds me of my mother."

"May I see?"

"Sure." She padded her way through the large foyer and down the long hallway into the kitchen. She pulled out a folder from her backpack and found the picture. "It's just weird."

Jacob swallowed. "Wow. The eyes are duller than all the pictures I've seen of your mom, but they *are* really similar."

"I know."

"What is this guy's name?"

"Edward Howell. Ring any bells?"

Jacob shook his head. But that didn't mean anything. "What was the name he gave you for his wife?"

"MaryAnn. Maiden name Grant. But again, he said that was bogus. He gave me this song and dance about how she ran from her family due to bad blood but said that he has no idea what it was, and he never pried. Not for twenty-seven or so fucking years." Katie found the whiskey bottle and poured herself a shot. She held it up.

Jacob shook his head. He wished he could join, but he still needed to go see his parents. "That seems a little odd."

"That's what I thought. I mean, if I were with a guy that long, I would want to know about all the skeletons in his closet."

"Agreed. But let's face it, you and I have learned firsthand that families keep secrets. They think it's for the greater good, but all it does is tear people apart."

"You've certainly forgiven your father for cheating on your mom." Katie raised her glass before downing it in one gulp.

"I wouldn't go that far." Jacob ran a hand through his hair. He should have stopped at the barbershop on the way home. His hair hadn't been this long since college. "But it happened a long time ago, and it's Mom's forgiveness that matters."

"I suppose you have a point there. But why in the hell is your dad still looking out for Owen?"

Jacob let out a long breath. "That, I have no answer for. But he's always been there for you."

"I know. However, with Owen living ten miles away, it just feels like a betrayal."

Taking a risk, Jacob reached out and palmed her cheek. Thankfully, she didn't shove his hand away. "I wish my father would drop him as a client. I've asked him too many times over the years. I don't get why he won't. I once asked my mother if it had to do with her, and she nearly bit my head off, but not because she was offended by my dad's actions. She was upset that I'd asked."

"I asked your father once. All he said was that, sometimes, there were things we didn't understand. And that he hoped someday we'd all find the truth. If I didn't have a lot of respect for your dad, I would have slapped him."

Jacob took her chin with his thumb and forefinger. He inched closer, his lips only inches from hers.

Her long lashes fluttered over her blue-green eyes. He held her gaze for a long moment before gently brushing his lips over her mouth in a tender kiss. He kept it light and pulled back after only a few seconds.

No way would he push his luck.

Katie could turn on someone in a split second.

"Why don't you send me whatever you have on this Edward guy, and I'll see if I can find anything? And scan in that picture. I'll see if it comes up in our database."

"I don't want you getting in trouble." She curled her finger around his biceps. "Before you go using the FBI database, let me see what I can come up with on my own. If I run into a dead-end, I'll let you know."

"Are you sure?"

"Yes. And I know you, Jacob." She lowered her chin. "Don't go doing it anyway. You already bend so many rules for Jackson and me. And we appreciate it, but let's save it for when we really need it. Like on the Williams case, okay?"

"Fair enough." He'd ignored her wishes a few times in the past.

That had been a big mistake. One he didn't plan to make again.

"But don't hesitate to ask me for help."

She smiled, dropping her hand to her side. "You know I won't. Now, get out of here and go see your parents. Don't be too late because I'll hear that rattly old truck of yours. You need a damn muffler. Better yet. A new vehicle."

"I actually bought a new truck yesterday. I pick it up in a couple of weeks." He kissed her cheek. "Lock up after me, got it?"

"Yes, sir."

Jacob turned off the headlights but kept the Jeep's motor running as he sat in the driveway of his childhood home. He stared at the picture of his older brother taped to his dash. Jacob had only been seven when Jonathon died. His memories from that day were still so fuzzy. His childhood therapist had told him that he might never remember all the details, and his parents didn't talk about it with him much—other than to discuss a few happy memories.

A light flickered on in the window above the garage. He watched his mother, Isabelle, slip on her smock and sit down in front of a canvas. She tucked her shoulder-length dark brown hair behind her ears before picking up the wooden paintbrush. She dipped it into some paint, held it about an inch from the canvas, then lowered her hand to her lap.

He watched her tilt her head. He knew she was examining the partially done picture. He smiled. His mother's art had gotten her through so much. In the early days following his brother's death, art had always pulled her back together when she was on the brink of falling apart.

Not her second son.

He didn't blame her for being distant. Losing a child had to be hard. But he always felt as though his mom was just as out of reach as his brother.

She glanced out the window. She immediately smiled and waved as she stood before disappearing into the house.

He glanced around the perfectly manicured yard, mentally counting the seconds it would take his mother to come open the garage. Or perhaps she'd call for Dad to do it.

The yard looked as it always did. Perfect. No one would ever find a single weed growing in his mother's garden. The grass always felt thick and plush against his bare feet. His father used only the best fertilizer. He also used only the highest quality machinery to keep the lawn looking brighter and better than any of the neighbors. Even in the winter, when most things died in upstate New York, his family home seemed to come alive with the extravagant decorations his mother was notorious for. She even decorated the pirate ship tree house to match each holiday.

Now, the yard was being prepared for the Fourth of July. The flag had already landed on the ship's mast, and the automated fireworks that lit up half the neighborhood at night occupied the sails.

The garage door hummed to life.

He could see his mother's feet. Actually, he saw her ugly green Crocs as she hurried toward the door, bending at the waist so he could see her. At least, she moved as if she were happy to see him. "Why on earth were you sitting in your car? Don't you have your key?" She tapped her foot, waiting for the garage door to lift over her head. She walked toward him with open arms.

He snagged the paperwork his father had asked him for and stepped from his Jeep.

She gave him a quick peck on the cheek and a few pats on the back.

"Hi, Mom," he said. "Did I disturb a masterpiece?"

"I was just going to touch up something I did for an old friend." She tilted her head. "You are in desperate need of a haircut."

"No comment." He took her by the hand and led her into the house. "You look beautiful." The aging process had been good to his mother. While she had a few wrinkles like the rest of the world, her blue eyes were brighter than ever. Hard to believe a world of darkness lived behind them.

"I raised you right," she said. "Let's go find your father."

All three cars in the garage were lined up perfectly on their painted tire tracks. Every tool was hung in its proper place. Not a speck of dirt anywhere. His parents would flip if they walked into the Bateman estate. He couldn't even argue that it was organized clutter.

He followed his mother into the glorified back foyer. To him, it was an entire room. To the right of the door was a solid oak bench that his grandfather had carved as a small boy. His mother had since refinished it and painted a swirling array of colors. An oval-shaped, tan leather chair with some oddly shaped floor lamp was situated directly across from the bench. He kicked off his shoes onto the rubber mat next to the oversized closet. It made his mother happy when everything was put in its perfect place.

His mother hung her smock on the coat hanger and then carefully removed her Crocs, exposing some kind of nylon stocking or something as she slipped her feet into her favorite pair of Ugg slippers.

"No socks?" his mother asked, hands on her hips. "That's just gross."

He kept his gaze on his feet and wiggled his toes against the cold tile floors that were identical in color to the dark brown leather furniture in the family room.

"Here." She shoved a pair of *guest slippers* under his nose. "Not only will they protect your soles, but they will also protect my floors and keep them from smelling like your stinky feet. You should really wear socks."

"Yes, ma'am."

"And when you leave here tonight, take the slippers with you."

"Where's dad?"

"Watching the ten-o'clock news."

Jacob pushed the swing door open and let his mother pass into the short hallway where the walls were painted a million different colors. In every room in the house, she had hand-painted something.

Raif, his father, lovingly called it *high-rent graffiti*. She had a real gift for color and design, though she sucked at doing portraits. Every year until he was about twelve, she would make him sit on a stool while she practiced. And every year, she'd say, *"Well, I don't think we want to save this one."* He was very thankful that his mother had discarded them all.

Over his mother's head, he saw his father stretched out in his chair with his slippered feet resting comfortably on the matching ottoman. "Hey, Dad," Jacob said.

"I thought I heard your Jeep in the driveway." His father turned down the volume and motioned for him to take a seat. "You need a new muffler."

"You'll be happy to know I bought a new truck."

"Finally," his father said.

"Yeah. I know." Jacob planted his butt in a chair that matched his father's, except for the color. His dad's was dark brown, while Jacob's was a shade or two lighter—or so his mother had pointed out once in great detail. Jacob and Raif had learned long ago never to disagree with Isabelle on color.

She was the expert.

"Can I get everyone something to drink?" his mother asked.

"Thanks, Mom, but I'm good. I can't stay long."

His father grabbed his no-spill coffee mug and held it up. "Did you bring me the documents?"

"That's one reason I came over." Jacob handed his dad the folder. "I called in a favor to get this for you. But you should know that the district attorney is coming after your client, guns blazing."

"I know. All I want is to get my client the best deal possible." His father set the paperwork on the table. "What was the other reason you stopped by?"

"Someone broke into the Bateman house."

"Were you or Katie there?" his father asked.

"No," Jacob said.

"How is Katie doing?" Isabelle settled herself into what the family referred to as the *reading throne*. It was an oversized chaise lounge, basically a chair with a built-in ottoman. She took the fuzzy blue blanket from the end table and covered her legs. "I always thought you and Katie made such a perfect couple," she said.

"Long time ago, Mom."

"Who do the cops think it was?" his father asked.

"Teenagers." Jacob stared at his father for a brief but intense moment. "Katie thinks it was her uncle."

Raif took a long, slow sip of his drink, almost ignoring the statement. "Not likely."

"Doesn't it bother you that he's only been out for two years and just rolls back into town a few months ago?"

"No," Raif said. "But it does bother me that my son is consumed by the rumors this town has been spreading instead of believing his dad."

"You've never given me any reason to believe you. Because you haven't told me anything. You haven't even denied any of it."

"Stop it," Isabelle said. "The past is in the past. Let's leave it there."

"Your mother's right." Raif set his mug on the end table, adjusting it slightly so it fit perfectly in the center of the coaster.

"Why? Because there are more lies to be uncovered?" Jacob cringed. Pushing his father's buttons was one thing. His mother's was an entirely different story.

"Don't blame your father for that lie. I didn't want you to know, and if that nosy reporter hadn't stuck her nose where it didn't belong, that ugliness wouldn't have been spread."

"Considering Owen's release two years ago, and then his move back here, this town has been all abuzz. Not to mention, they never found a body, and there are still a few million dollars missing," Jacob said. "I think Dad's indiscretion would have come out eventually."

"Perhaps the world should focus on finding the real killer," Isabelle said, "and stop gossiping about something that is frankly none of their business." She folded her arms across her chest and stared Jacob down as if he'd insulted her sensibilities.

Jacob opened his mouth but then shut it tight before saying something he knew he would regret later. His parents had always claimed that Owen had been wrongly accused of everything, but they could never really give Jacob a solid reason. The fact that his parents were still hiding some dark secret from the world didn't bother him. It was the fact that they were hiding it from their son that made him crazy.

"Was there anything else you wanted?" his father asked.

"I'm worried about your safety," Jacob said.

"You think Owen is a danger to us?" Raif stared, unblinking, but with a mocking upturn of his lips.

"The past is full of mistakes and bad choices," his mother said. "We can't go back and change them. And I, for one, have learned that holding onto them only makes us incapable of having any kind of future—much less a here and now. Anyone want apple pie?"

Jacob tried not to laugh. That was his mother's answer to everything, especially when the topic was clearly moving in the direction of things that reminded her of the dark years after Jonathon had died. "No thanks on the pie, Ma. And for the record, I just want you two to take extra precautions. I know he was your friend, but he's dangerous."

"We will make sure we lock up tight," his mother said. Jacob wasn't surprised by how she seemed to dismiss the danger. "You should be helping Katie," his mother continued. "I know she is still mad at your father and me for lying to her all those years, but we thought we were protecting her. And you."

"Protect yourselves from Owen. He killed once; he could do it again."

A long moment of silence passed. His parents shared a glance and seemed to communicate something between them.

"We'll be cautious," his father said. "But I want you to remember one thing, and maybe consider doing something."

"What's that?"

"It's almost impossible to convict without a body and—"

"I'm not allowed anywhere near those case files. But you are, and even you won't let me see them."

"Perhaps I've changed my mind on that," his father said.

"Raif. That's not a good idea," his mother added.

Well, *that* was interesting. "Are you saying you'll give them to me? Including what wasn't allowed into evidence?" Jacob asked. "Because I've read all the public records, and from what I've seen, the district attorney had more than enough to get a solid conviction for embezzling from his family's foundation. From his own sister and niece. They followed the paper trail to some offshore bank accounts with Owen's name on them, and he withdrew all the money the day Grace disappeared."

"The day she was murdered. But not by Owen," Raif said as he drew his lips tight.

"I don't want to argue. I just want you to be careful." This was not the right time to get into this argument.

"We always are," his mother said. "But you really don't need to worry about Owen. He got a raw deal, and I wish we could prove it."

There was no talking to his parents about this. But he would press his father about the files tomorrow.

"I'll walk you to your truck," his father said.

Jacob followed his dad through the house and out to the Jeep. The dark clouds covered all the stars and the moon. The only thing Jacob could see was his breath.

"I'll give you the files on one condition," his father said. "You don't tell Katie."

"Dad. I'm not sure I can do that."

"Then I won't give them to you."

Jacob pinched the bridge of his nose. "If Owen didn't kill Grace, then who did?"

"That's the million-dollar question. I've been trying to figure it out for twenty-seven years and have come up blank every time. But I suspect it might be tied to whoever Katie's father is. A question that has never been answered. Has she ever brought that up with you?"

Jacob shook his head. That was a sore subject with Katie. "She doesn't like to talk about it."

"I know. I've asked her if she ever wants to try to find out who he is, but the answer is always the same."

"If her mother wanted her to know, she would have told her," Jacob repeated the words that Katie had said to him a million times. "But she was so young. She barely remembers her mom."

"Or that night." His father rubbed his chin. "I did the best I could to protect her. To keep her from the spotlight and away from reporters and being questioned by doctors and the police."

"I know you did, Dad. And so does she. But that doesn't change the fact that you defended Owen. Relentlessly. And he was found guilty."

"That doesn't mean he did it. And you know it." Raif moved a little closer. "I make more plea bargains than I go to court. I know I work for a lot of people that belong behind bars. But that doesn't mean they don't have rights."

Jacob had heard this speech a million times and knew there was no point in interrupting the old man.

"However, when I know in my gut that the client didn't do what they are accused of, I will go to bat for them. Owen didn't do this."

"Dad. He lost every appeal. It took two parole hearings before they let him out. That says something."

"It says I didn't do my job and failed my best friend." Tears welled in his eyes. "Owen has been doing his own digging. Maybe you and Katie—"

"No. Show me your files first. Let me see what wasn't allowed into evidence on Owen's behalf, and then maybe I'll take a look at what Owen has."

"I can live with that." His father glanced over his shoulder. "The anniversary of your brother's death is coming up soon."

"I know."

"Your mother loves you. She just really struggles this time of year."

She struggled at every holiday, and no amount of his father's justifications would make up for his mother's lack of affection.

Except for maybe the fact that his father had always been there for him when it counted most.

"I know that, too." He pulled his father in for a hug. "I'll make sure I come around more often."

"Thanks. I appreciate that."

Jacob climbed behind the steering wheel and waited for his father to close the garage door before backing out of the driveway.

He'd gotten more out of his dad in an hour than he had in the last two years.

3

*K*atie jogged down the stairs carrying a frame she'd found in one of the many rooms upstairs. She rounded the corner into the kitchen and paused mid-step.

Jacob peered over the paper. "Good morning."

"What are you still doing here?" She glanced at her watch. It was only seven, but he was usually out the door by now.

"I wanted to talk to you before I left."

"Okay. But follow me to the patio. I want to put my mother's picture in this."

"Sure thing." Jacob stood. He'd yet to put on his tie and suit coat. He usually saved that for when he made it to the office.

She tried not to check out his nice ass as he sauntered through the house, but it proved impossible. He was tall and lean and sexy as hell. She often wished she could get past their history.

It wasn't just what he'd done.

She struggled with personal demons, as well, and hadn't been very nice to Jacob, all because of who his family was. And she wasn't sure if she could ever get past that fact.

Katie admired the picture of her mother as she hung it back on the wall in its new frame. Her mom wore a sundress, and her long, red hair flowed behind her shoulders. Katie wished she knew when the picture had been taken. There weren't many, and she cherished every one.

She opened a few windows. The birds chirped, welcoming the morning. A few boats hummed along the shore. She took a slow breath in through her nose, letting the crisp, cool air expand her lungs. The morning sun barely peeked over the horizon, casting a white glare across the sky and lake. She loved to watch the way the blues slowly pushed away the blackness of night. Since she could remember, dawn had always been her favorite time.

"So, what's on your mind?"

"Your uncle, for one."

"What about him?" Katie took a seat in the swing, letting the cool breeze tickle her skin. Before she and Jacob had broken up, they used to take his boat out and go camping. It was one of her fondest memories of their time together. For some reason, this reminded her of that.

"Do you think he knows who your father is?"

Katie coughed. "We've talked about this before."

"Actually, we haven't. At least, not about Owen possibly knowing." Jacob had asked his parents a few times, and they'd always said they had no idea. That no one did except Grace, and she'd never told anyone.

"I don't know. I've never asked him."

"Because you haven't talked to him since you were four years old." Jacob sat on the rocking chair.

She closed her eyes and listened to the squeaky chair, focusing on the rhythmic sound. "And why should I?"

"Because my father said something interesting to me last night."

She peeked open one eye and turned her head. "I'm probably going to regret asking what on earth Raif Donovan had to say, but bring it on."

"He believes the key to finding your mother is finding out who your father is."

Katie laughed. "So, your dad believes that my biological father killed my mom and stole the money?"

"That's what Dad implied."

"What about the rumors that my mother left home when she was young and was a sex worker and that the end result was me? No one ever denied those rumors, including your parents." Katie couldn't stand the rumor mill. And Hannah, the wonder reporter, enjoyed stirring the pot every chance she got.

"Because no one knows."

"Your father had an affair with my mom. You'd think she'd confide in him about something like that." Katie's pulse increased. She needed to stop bringing that up. All it did was hurt Jacob, and she needed to stop doing that if she ever wanted to repair their relationship so they could be friends.

At the very least, she wanted that.

She didn't believe they could ever be more. Not right now, anyway. Wow. Where did that thought come from?

"I can't say I've ever talked to my dad about that, either," he said. "I wasn't going to tell you this because I don't know if my old man will follow through or not, but I might be able to take a peek at his files from the case."

She bolted to her feet. "You'd better share those with me."

"And that's why I wasn't going to tell you."

She grabbed him by his shirt and yanked him to his feet. "Jacob Nathaniel Donovan. If you get any of the private notes, records, or evidence that wasn't logged into public record and don't at least give me a summary, I will not only kick your sorry ass out of my house and not let you dock your boat here. Not to mention, I will never speak to you again."

He curled his fingers around her wrists. "If there is

anything in them worth sharing, I promise you will know."

"Once upon a time, you believed me. What changed?" She tilted her head. Her entire life, Jacob had been her confidant. Her best friend. The one person she could count on, no matter what. She knew that she was mostly at fault for the demise of their relationship, but he was the one who'd started questioning whether or not Owen was guilty.

Not her.

"I've never stopped believing you," he whispered. "Only, there are too many unanswered questions."

She leaned into his strong body, allowing her desire to take over her good senses. She should back away, but she couldn't. The need to feel his lips against hers was greater than the need to protect her heart.

A moan developed deep in her throat. She'd forgotten what a passionate kisser he was, and how he could melt away her worries.

She jumped when her phone vibrated in her back pocket. Her forehead smacked his nose.

"Ouch." He groaned.

"Shit. Sorry." She held up her cell. "Jackson is on his way over. He says it's important. Something about my uncle."

"I'll stick around until he gets here."

"You don't have to do that," she said.

"I want to." He rubbed his hands up and down her

forearms. "I want to know what's going on with him. I don't trust him as far as I can spit."

"Me, neither," she mumbled. "Would you like some more coffee?"

"As a matter of fact, I would."

She practically raced through the house, hoping he didn't follow. Why the hell did she have to go and kiss Jacob? Knowing him, he'd take that as a sign that things were moving past the friend zone, only they were barely in that zone to begin with.

Nervously, she moved about the kitchen, making a large pot of brew. She pulled out the toaster, deciding food might calm her nerves, as well. Anything to keep her occupied so she didn't have to be alone with Jacob. Once Jackson was here, she'd be safe from herself. And then Jacob would leave, not to return until late, and she'd make sure she was in her room, ignoring him.

She didn't need to find herself in a lip-lock again. It was all too familiar territory. Being back in his arms might feel good—and maybe even right. But they had no future.

Her phone buzzed just as Jacob came flying through the kitchen. "What's got your panties in a wad?" she asked.

"Jackson's at the garage door."

"He's got the code," she said.

"I know. But Owen is down the street."

Her heart dropped to the pit of her stomach. "You've got to be kidding me." She swallowed. Her uncle had a lot of fucking balls showing up at the end of Rockhurst Road. It was a dead-end street, essentially trapping the man. Not too bright.

She followed Jacob into the garage and paused as her pulse became lodged in her throat. "He's crazy." She stared at her uncle, leaning against his vehicle with his arms folded across his chest.

"I'd have to agree," Jacob whispered. "I wonder if my old man knows what his client is up to."

"If he knew, I hope he at least advised against it," Jackson said. "This could be seen as intimidation."

She inched closer to the edge of the driveway as she tried to conjure up memories of her mother. Unfortunately, she had very few. Partial visions wove in and out of her mind as she reached in to pluck a real memory from the hidden recesses of her brain. The moving pictures she imagined were more like stick figures that came to life, but they were hers, and she cherished them.

She stopped at the edge of the street and clutched the locket dangling from her neck. She glanced to the side yard, and tears welled in her eyes. All her life, she'd had this dream of racing across this grassy patch with a handful of flowers stolen from the neighbors' yard. She'd hand them to her mother, who would smile proudly while patting her on the head. She had no idea if the dream was real or some figment of her imagination, but it was the one constant in her life, and it comforted her.

Katie looked to the left. A sailboat tacked about fifty feet from shore. A warmth rolled over the skin of her hands. She rubbed them together, trying to forget the sweet memory of sitting on the dock with her uncle as she kicked her little feet in the water, counting the boats as they came out of Sandy Bay.

This was a memory that felt more real than any other, and it angered her because she'd felt safe and more protected with Owen than anyone else that she could remember.

"I'm going to go talk to him," she said.

"Not without one of us, you're not." Jacob squeezed her hand. "And since he knows me, I think I should go."

"I agree," Jackson said. "I'll hang back and observe."

The sun continued its steady climb as she and Jacob made their way down the long driveway. Her heart hammered in her chest, and if it weren't for Jacob and Jackson, she'd probably go off half-cocked.

Which wouldn't help matters.

Or get information.

"I have a mind to call the cops." She stopped about twenty feet from her uncle.

"I'm not doing anything wrong," he said. He shoved his hands deep into his jeans' pockets. He wore a red hoodie sweatshirt. Very different from the suit and ties he wore when he was once a well-respected psychiatrist.

"You're trespassing," she said.

"I'm on a public road, not your property."

"I don't care," she said, taking in slow breaths. "You're not welcome here."

"Does my father know you decided to intimidate Katie?" Jacob asked.

Owen let out a dry laugh. "That's a strong word, son." His hair was whiter, and he had deep wrinkles around his eyes. He looked old and worn. "I don't mean anyone any harm."

"That's probably what you told me when you locked me in the freezer." It was impossible not to look him directly in his bright blue eyes. They were still kind and welcoming. Everyone who knew him way back when always said he was kind, sweet, and generous.

"I never locked you in any freezer." He held up his hands. "I know my prints were all over that appliance. But so were your mother's. Not to mention another set that was never allowed into evidence."

She stole a glance at Jacob, who arched a brow.

"I see that's news to you," Owen said. "I heard the estate was broken into last night."

"Really? And you know that because you're the one who broke in," Katie said.

Owen shook his head. "That wasn't me. But that's what brings—"

"Oh, of course, it wasn't you. How foolish of me to think otherwise. Now, tell me where my mother's body is buried and where all *my* money is, and we'll call it even."

Owen swiped at his face as if he might produce

tears. "I wish I could do that. But I have no idea. I was drugged that night. I don't remember anything."

"You're still sticking to that story?" Katie squeezed Jacob's hand even harder.

"It's not a story, and I'm worried you're in danger. That whatever happened to your mother will happen to you."

Jacob stepped forward. "Are you threatening her? Because—"

Owen held up his hands. "No. No. I'm not a threat to you. But I fear that my being out of prison has set off a chain of events that we don't understand. All I've ever wanted was to protect you. It's why I went to prison."

"Excuse me?" Jacob said. "What the hell does that mean?"

"I know I didn't kill Grace. So, whoever did is still out there. At the end of the day, I figured with me gone, they wouldn't come back. But now that I'm out, a few strange things have been happening."

"Are you having a psychotic break? Does he have a name? Is there more than one personality I should be worried about?" Katie had always wondered why Owen hadn't used that as a defense. It wasn't like mental health issues didn't run rampant in their family.

"You can joke all you want, but understand that your safety could be in jeopardy." He kept his gaze locked on hers. "Keep your eyes open, and if you see even one little thing out of whack, any weird happenings, contact Raif and tell him. He'll know what to do."

"Why is my father protecting you?" Jacob asked with a strained voice. "What do you have on him? Or does he owe you? I don't get it."

"If we had all the answers, Katie wouldn't be looking at me with fear and hatred in her eyes." Owen looked past her. "Who's that in the garage?"

"Meet my partner, Jackson. Now, I think I've entertained this conversation a little too long. Leave, or I'll call the cops."

"Be safe and watch your back," Owen said.

"Still sounds like a threat to me." Katie clenched her fists, doing her best to keep her rage in check. Seeing him, here, like this, was hard enough. The idea that she could wrap her fingers around his neck and squeeze the life out of him and possibly enjoy it was terrifying. "Leave now," she said.

He pushed himself from the car and started to walk around to the driver's side. He got in and started the engine.

Katie felt Jacob pull her close to his side. His arm wrapped protectively around her body made her want to melt into his embrace and weep, but she wouldn't. Instead, she sucked in every ounce of strength he had to offer. She watched as Owen made a U-turn and headed toward the main road.

Jacob kissed her temple. "I'm going to call my father about this."

"Thanks. I appreciate that." She glanced up, catching his gaze.

He brushed his lips over hers in a soft, tender kiss. It lingered longer than it should, but she no longer cared. She needed something that made her feel alive, and that's exactly what Jacob did in the moment.

Jackson cleared his throat. "I did call the cops."

"Nothing they can do," Katie said.

"Not true. He keeps coming around, we use the system and file harassment charges. That should give him a few months in the slammer," Jacob said. "And let's not forget, a federal agent lives on the premises. We can milk that. I'm going to talk to my supervisor and find out exactly what we can do because Owen's words...they were fighting words." Jacob rested his hand on the small of her back, nudging her toward the garage.

"I don't want him in jail until I know where he left my mother," she said.

"Be reasonable, Katie. The man tried to kill you," Jacob said.

"Don't you think I know that?" She took a step back. "Look at me." She held out her shaking hands. "I'm terrified of that man, and I want him put away for the rest of his life this time. But until that happens, I want him to lead me to my mother. She deserves a proper burial. She deserves a place where we can all remember..." Slowly, she raised her hand and fingered the locket. "He's going to show me. Killers like him always do."

Jacob shook his head. "Babe, I understand, I do. But be rational. We're all safer if he's locked up."

"I don't want to argue, and you need to get to work," she said.

Jacob glanced at his watch. "Shit. I'm late." He gave her one more kiss, and she didn't stop him. "Keep an eye on her, got it?"

"Will do," Jackson said with a wicked grin.

Katie groaned. The last thing she wanted was to hear anything out of Jackson's mouth about her having a little kissy-face time with Jacob.

But she knew it was coming.

Jacob raced through the house, grabbing his backpack, tie, and coat, before climbing into his Jeep and driving off.

Katie tried to ignore Jackson as he sat at the kitchen table, eating a bagel and smiling like a stupid kid who had just been told he could stay up past his bedtime.

"Stop staring at me," she said.

"Would you rather I pick on you?"

"No." She leaned against the counter and picked at her bagel. "What do you think about what just happened?"

"I find it interesting that there were three prints on the freezer, but one set was not admissible. It actually makes no sense."

"Maybe they were mine."

"I suppose, but unless someone gives us those files, we may never know."

She chewed on her food for a long moment. "Jacob might have access to them. But he's not sure yet. You know his dad. He can be fickle and change his mind."

"Even more interesting," Jackson said.

"Jacob wants to nail Owen, and not just because of me. He wants to put the lid on the rumors once and for all."

"I think you and Jacob put more stock in all that than anyone else," Jackson said.

"Finding out that his father had an affair with my mother pretty much broke Jacob's heart."

"I imagine it would. But it was a long time ago, and his parents seem to have rebounded. So should the two of you," Jackson said. "You really should forgive Jacob. He's a good guy, and I know he still cares about you."

"It's not a matter of forgiving him anymore." She stared at the ceiling as if it had all the answers. Instead, she found a spider that needed killing. "We were basically broken up when he slept with Hannah. And I can almost understand why he did it. I wasn't the nicest person to him during the last few months we were together."

"Then what's the problem?"

"After we found out about the affair, I told him that I bet he would turn out just like his father and that I couldn't love a man like that. When I found out he'd slept with Hannah, I told him that he'd proven my point."

"Ouch," Jackson said. "And it's a lie."

"Yeah. But let's not forget that it was Hannah who broke the news about our parents' sordid little romp in the sack. That changed things for us. Changed them forever."

"It doesn't have to be that way." Jackson had been like the big brother she'd never had. The idea of not having him in her life was a concept she couldn't wrap her brain around, in the same way she knew she'd never love anyone the way she loved Jacob.

"We are better as friends. We both know that."

"You can tell yourself that little lie all you want," Jackson said. "But what I just witnessed today, was two people who still have deep feelings for each other.

4

Jacob pressed his fingers against his temple and rubbed in a circular motion as he waited for his father to pick up the damn phone. His receptionist had said that it wouldn't be but a few minutes. Jacob glanced at his watch. Eight minutes, to be exact.

"Sorry, son. One of the associates stuck their head in my office."

Likely story. "No problem."

"What do you need? It must be important for you to wait more than a few minutes for me."

"It's urgent," Jacob said. "Owen showed up at Katie's house today."

"Oh. I didn't know that."

"Well, you should know that we called the cops, and I have a meeting with my superior about what we can do since I live there, too. He said some pretty threatening things."

"I doubt that," his father said with a bit of a snicker. "If anything, he's concerned for Katie's safety, and you both twisted it out of your hatred for the man—which I understand. But you have to trust me that he's not a danger to Katie. Or anyone for that matter."

Jacob had replayed the conversation with Owen over in his head a dozen times during his drive, and he hated to admit that his father might be correct about how he and Katie had heard what they wanted to. But still. Owen was a convicted murderer. "Dad, you've never given me any real reason to believe you. All the evidence I've seen—though I agree much was circumstantial, and I have to admit, you didn't fight as hard for your client as you usually do—points to Owen."

"Owen was set up," his father said. "I've been trying to find a way to prove it for twenty-seven years. But the only other person we could ever come up with as a possible suspect was Grace—"

"That makes no sense. That would mean she's still alive somewhere." He leaned back in his chair and stared at the ceiling. He closed his eyes for a long moment, letting his father's statement sink in. "Why would she do that?" He couldn't believe that he was even entertaining this conversation. But what was even more interesting was that his father was finally explaining himself to someone.

"She wouldn't leave Katie behind. Not a second time."

Jacob blinked his eyes open as he bolted upright. "Excuse me. What the hell does that mean? Katie has never mentioned that to me."

"She probably doesn't know. And if I were you, I wouldn't tell her just yet."

Jacob blew out a puff of air. Keeping secrets from Katie wasn't a good way to get back in her good graces and win her affection. "I won't lie to her," Jacob said. "Now, tell me what the hell happened."

"How about you stop by the office or at home and we can chat?"

"And the files?"

"I'll get you a copy on one condition," his father said.

"I take it you still don't want me to show them to Katie." Jacob hated it when his old man required some sort of return favor. It would usually either get Jacob into trouble or be something he didn't want to do.

Both equally bad.

"I know I can't stop you once I show them to you, but you need to be careful with the contents. And let's face it, Katie tends to go off half-cocked. Maybe you should look through them alone and then discuss with me how best to go about feeding Katie the intel."

"That's a big ask, Dad, and I don't think a good one."

"Why?"

Jacob set his elbow on the desk and pinched his

nose. If he told his father the truth, he'd never hear the end of it.

If he lied, his dad might actually withhold the paperwork.

"Because I still love her, and I'm trying to find a way to make things right again. If I keep this from her, she'll never forgive me. And I wouldn't blame her."

"Why don't you tell me something I don't know?" his father said. "However, she's so angry right now. And she's so hyper-focused, I'm afraid she can't see past that. If you still don't believe us after you see everything, then so be it."

"Let me ask you this…" Jacob let out a long breath. A slow, dull ache crept up from the back of his neck, making its way across the top of his head. "Why now? Why didn't you bring this to me years ago? Or when Owen first got out?"

"Owen didn't want me to. He's always believed that if he was in jail, Katie was safe. He's always thought that once he got out, whoever killed Grace would come back."

"Why does he believe that?" The more Jacob talked to his father, the less he understood.

"About six months before Grace died, she started behaving erratically."

"That's when you had an affair with her."

His father let out a dry chuckle. "I never slept with Grace."

Jacob stuck his finger in his ear and gave it a good

wiggle. "If that's true, why are you letting the world believe that?"

"Owen thought it would help keep Katie safe."

"Dad. That makes no fucking sense at all. And what about Mom? I can't believe she would go along with this."

"First, it makes a lot of sense. And second, your mother knows everything."

Jacob's chest tightened. His mother had always been so distant. She wasn't cold, not at all. She'd been affectionate, always hugging him and reading to him, but there were times she was just…absent. He knew his older brother's death, and the fact that she still blamed herself, had done a number on her, but the idea that she knew her husband had never cheated but allowed the rumor to perpetuate didn't seem real.

"You need to understand that Owen and I both knew that Grace was seeing someone during that time. But she wouldn't tell anyone about him or bring him around. And whoever this man was, he made her more jittery than usual. She was being secretive, and she withdrew a ton of money from her trust a week before she died," his father said.

"How much?"

"Five hundred thousand," his father said.

"That was never brought up in trial."

"Besides being deemed inadmissible, it was another thing Owen thought was better left out of it."

"You make it sound like Owen *wanted* to go to jail."

"He did," his father said. "Look. I've got a meeting, and I'm going to be tied up for most of the day."

"Me, too. Maybe I can stop by the house tonight. Or first thing in the morning."

"Sounds good," his father said. "And I know you want to read Katie in on everything, but just remember what a little firecracker she is, and that she doesn't always think before she speaks."

Jacob didn't need a lesson on his ex-girlfriend. "I'll text you later. Love you, Dad."

"Love you, too, son."

The line went dead.

Jacob rubbed his temple and stared at the case files on his desk. He'd been staring at them for three hours, and nothing had changed except that Cassidy Williams had gone from a missing person's case to an unsolved murder. According to the LAPD, there were no leads, but they'd officially called in the FBI for assistance, bringing in the Violent Crimes Unit, which technically took Jacob off the case. However, since he'd uncovered some cold cases that fit *The Doe Hunter's* profile, he was being retained as a consultant.

He pulled out a picture of Cassidy. She had red hair and had been murdered with a bow and arrow. According to the autopsy report, she had been dehydrated when they found her, and her skin was severely sunburned. Everything fit *The Doe Hunter*'s profile. And to date, the FBI had linked at least five dead girls and a dozen missing others to this killer that spanned three decades.

Jacob could sense Cameron, the boy genius, standing at the doorway. "This is your office, too. You don't need my permission to enter."

"Actually, I'm watching."

"Watching what? Dare I ask?" Jacob liked Cameron, but his social skills were lacking.

"You. Trying to figure out how your brain works," Cameron said. "I've heard you're the smartest guy in this place."

"Second smartest." Jacob leaned back, rolling his shoulders and trying to relax. The knots in his back would take at least two hours for even a good massage therapist to work out. "I've heard my new partner is scary-smart."

Cameron entered the office and sat behind his desk. "There is a difference between book smart—me—and street smart—you."

"Not true," Jacob said. "You have to trust your instincts. They are spot-on. Stop looking at what the textbooks and psychology professors tell you and start applying what your gut says. The textbooks are your base, your gut is your guide."

"Is that what you did?"

Jacob laughed. "I'm not that smart. I'm just cocky."

"I don't buy that," Cameron said. "I did some checking into those files—"

A knock at the door cut him off. It was Cindy.

"Come in," Jacob said. "What can I do for you today, lovely?"

She dropped a bunch of files on his desk. "More information from the Violent Crimes Unit on *The Doe Hunter*. They are sending a victim profiler up here to speak with her parents tomorrow. They invited you to be present for that interview."

"That's awesome. Do we have a time set up yet?"

"I'm waiting to hear from the parents. I'll let you know."

"Is that all?" Jacob asked.

Cindy stood in the doorway, hesitant to leave, but seemingly even more reluctant to speak whatever was on her mind.

"Well?" Jacob prodded.

"I just came from Capri's. And, well, your dad was there."

"My dad is in Albany? That can't be. I spoke to him a few hours ago. He was in his office in Saratoga. He had appointments all day. Are you sure?"

Cindy nodded. "But he wasn't inside. She glanced over at Cameron then back to Jacob. "Maybe you want to go over there and see what's going on."

"Maybe I want you to just spill it," Jacob said.

"He was in a beat-up old sedan in a parking lot with Owen Bateman."

His father generally didn't meet Owen anywhere but in his office—or at least that's what his old man had always told him. So, why in a parking lot as if he had something to hide? Especially forty minutes from the law firm and an hour from home.

"Guess I'm going for a slice of pizza." Jacob pushed his chair back and snagged his sport coat. This was something he needed to see.

"You want me to go with?" Cameron asked.

"Nope. I want you going through those files. Categorize and make notes," he said as he made a beeline for the elevator.

The ride down had to be the slowest he'd ever experienced. He took out his phone, and as soon as he hit the main floor, he started punching in his father's number. Before he hit the last button, he thought better of tipping off his dad. He looked at his watch. It would take him at least ten minutes to walk to the diner, and twice as long just to get his car out of the parking garage.

The downtown Albany streets were cluttered with people, all seemingly conversing with themselves as they talked into their cell phones or headphones. Even though the sun was bright in the blue sky, it had started its descent.

He didn't bother walking to the corner before crossing the street. A few angry drivers honked their horns as he dogged between the slow-moving vehicles. He headed north, nearly jogging.

Just as he made it to the parking lot, he saw his father head inside. No sign of Owen, but Jackson's car was parked across the street. Once again, he dogged a few pissed-off drivers and dashed toward Katie, who sat in the passenger seat with her ugly green Jets cap parked on top of her head, hiding her beautiful red hair.

She didn't flinch when he pulled open the driver's side door.

"Jackson just went to use the bathroom so don't get too comfortable."

"No worries." Jacob shut the door. "So, whom are we spying on?"

"As if you didn't know." She glanced at him, her soft blue-green eyes showing the compassion she always had along with a hint of the love he'd once known. His heart beat a little faster. "I saw Cindy here about twenty minutes ago."

"Where'd Owen go?"

She lifted her cell phone. "Last report is that good ol' Uncle O is on the Northway."

"So, what were they doing?"

"I don't really know," she said. "My guy informed me that your father showed up about ten minutes after Owen did and got into Owen's car. They talked for about forty-five minutes. By the time I got here, your dad was walking across the parking lot, and Owen was driving off."

Jacob leaned his head against the headrest and

closed his eyes. "I'm going to tell you something that I promised my dad just a few hours ago I wouldn't."

"I don't like the sound of that."

"I need you to keep your cool and not shoot off your mouth, okay?" He turned his head and caught her gaze.

"Who, me? Never."

He laughed. "My dad said he never slept with your mom."

"They why didn't he deny it? And, come on, if I didn't believe my mom was cheating, you know I'd be scratching everyone's eyes out."

He cringed, remembering the day Katie had unleashed on him over sleeping with Hannah after he and Katie had already broken up. "My father claims that Grace was seeing a mystery man."

"Let me guess. That mystery man is who they believe killed my mom."

"That's a possibility. And they thought the longer Owen was in jail, the less likely this guy would be to return and finish you off." Jacob pressed his finger over her lips. "Sometime in the next twenty-four hours, I'm meeting with my old man to discuss this and take a look at his files from the trial. That should shed some light on all of this."

"You know where my mind just went, right?" Katie arched a brow.

"I get it. Whoever killed your mother tried to kill you, too. And who benefited most? Owen, because he'd get all the money." Jacob leaned in and stole a quick kiss. Not just to keep Katie from opening her mouth but also because he wanted to feel her soft lips against his. "Unless Grace secretly married someone."

"Is that the spin your father is putting on it?"

Jacob shook his head. "If someone else is behind this, they went to great lengths to set up your uncle. And let's face it, he went away on murder charges without a body and only a lot of circumstantial evidence. We both know that's true, so don't deny it. We're not kids anymore."

"I will admit that your dad did a pretty shitty job of representing my uncle, but I always wanted to believe it was because he knew he was guilty."

"What if we had that backward, and it was Owen who wanted it that way?"

"That's pretty heavy, and I'm not sure I can wrap my brain around that just yet."

"All right. Let me toss something else at you that jumped into my head." He pointed toward the news truck parked down the street.

"It's been there since we got here," Katie said. "I just hope that's not Hannah's crew."

"Speak of the devil." Jacob always hated bringing up the woman he'd had a short affair with, but he got the feeling she might have been a pawn in a game they knew nothing about. "Nobody knew about the affair until Hannah uncovered it, and that happened right around your uncle's first parole hearing."

"I really don't hate anyone. Except that bitch," Katie said under her breath. "And she's had it in for me."

"That's true. But what if someone fed her that detail?"

"Like who?"

"That's the million-dollar question." Jacob let out a breath.

"There's Jackson. We need to meet a client, which is why we were on our way down here in the first place." She adjusted her Jets cap. "I've got a weird feeling about this guy."

"Why?"

"He was supposed to bring us some pictures of his wife from when she was younger, but he kept putting us off. Today, he said that either he could mail them from Vegas because he was catching a flight to Atlanta tonight to visit some friends—which is weird by itself when his wife is missing. Or we could drive down here and get them."

"Where are you meeting him? Here?"

"Yep. And he's been sitting in his car ever since I got here." She pointed down the road from the parking lot of the restaurant. She tapped her cell. "We were supposed to meet five minutes ago, but he hasn't budged."

"He's probably waiting for you."

"He didn't seem like the type of guy who minds sitting alone." She leaned across the jeep, opened the glove box, and pulled out a small envelope. "I know I'm distrusting and paranoid at times."

"There's a lot going on right now."

"Finding out that Cassidy Williams was murdered put me over the edge."

"We think Cassidy was murdered by a serial killer we've just linked with a few other cases. It's big. Ted Bundy big."

"That's scary. I hope you nail the bastard."

"Yeah. Me, too. Especially since all the victims have red hair," he said.

She arched a brow. "I didn't need to know that."

"Yes, you did. And I sent Jackson a text message with the same information. You need to watch your back. You're a bit older than the victims so far, but still. That said, something else has you wigged out. What is it?"

She handed him the envelope.

"What's this?" he asked.

"Just open the envelope."

Jacob did as instructed. "Wow. She's got your eyes." He had to do a double-take between the photograph and Katie.

"Creepy, isn't it?"

"Who is this woman?" He studied the picture, forcing himself to ignore the intense familiarity of the light blue eyes and focus on the rest of the woman, who had spent way too much time in the sun.

"My client's missing wife."

"Weird."

"I agree," she said. "I'm hoping he gives us pictures of her from when she was younger, so I get that weird feeling out of my head. It's so fucking unsettling."

He reached out and palmed her cheek. "Your client is on the move."

"And Jackson is standing outside the truck."

"And my phone is vibrating." He pulled it out and read a text from Cameron. "I have to go. My new partner found something interesting on the case we're working."

"How's that going?"

"He's a good kid." While stuffing his phone into his pocket, he leaned in and kissed her on the cheek.

"You'd better get back to work," she said.

He smiled. "See you at home."

"If I'm awake."

"If I have files, I'm sure you will be." He winked, but before she could say anything, he jumped from her vehicle, waved to Jackson, and raced down the street. Work might be crazy, but it appeared his love life might be looking up.

Katie stepped from what she lovingly called Jackson's *daddy vehicle*. She'd never thought he'd trade in his pickup for a full-size SUV, but he wore *family man* well.

"I take it Jacob learned of his father's presence in the parking lot?"

"He did," Katie admitted. But she didn't feel like being razzed by Jackson so she moved the conversation to the issue at hand. "Do we have any other information on this Edward Howell guy?"

"Not much turned up in Vegas on either him or his wife. For rich people, they seem to live a very quiet existence. He does do a fair amount of gambling in the casinos, but he keeps a low profile. I didn't find anything, anywhere, about major winnings, but that doesn't mean anything. My contacts said MaryAnn kept to herself. Didn't socialize a lot, and Edward did a lot of traveling. She rarely went with him."

"What did she do when he was gone?"

"Not much. She didn't really have any friends from what I've been able to find out so far," Jackson said. "She's a bit of an enigma."

"What about pictures? Articles on him? Her? Anything?"

"No. Everything points to a simple, quiet life. No domestic disputes. Traffic violations. Nothing. Our client appears to be clean. A little *too* clean if you ask me, but we're also in a business that doesn't encourage trusting people in general."

She paused before going up the concrete walkway to the entrance. "So, you also think something is off with this guy?"

"I don't believe he's been honest with us about why

she left, but other than that, I think you're being a bit paranoid because of your uncle."

"You're probably right." Things with Edward didn't add up, but she was so immersed in her uncle and Jacob, she couldn't even deal with the current case.

She stepped into the diner and scanned the room, taking note of everyone in the place. On the right side was a young couple near the front door, sharing homefries. Two suits in the booth next to the kids. The next few booths were empty. Then back in the corner was Hannah Madison, the reporter, with two of her crewmen.

"We both knew it could be her that was here," Jackson whispered. "Don't start anything."

"Not planning on it. But I can't be responsible for what she does." Katie and Hannah silently acknowledged that they'd seen each other, but Katie's pulse went into double-time, wondering what Hannah might have seen in the parking lot. Hannah was a cut-throat reporter and didn't care who she stepped on to get her next story. Katie did her best to ignore Hannah's presence, at least for the time being. She fully intended to find a reason to grill the reporter later.

Regardless of Jackson said.

Lingering construction workers filled the counter space, but the other side of the diner was empty. Except for Edward.

Katie smiled and nodded as she made her way across the restaurant. Edward stood and returned the nod. He wore a black T-shirt and black pants. His keys, iPhone, and an envelope were on the table. "Good afternoon," he said.

"Sorry we're late." Katie slid across the vinyl booth. She didn't like the idea of having her back to the door, but she didn't have much choice.

"I just got here myself," Edward said. "I took a few wrong turns."

"Albany can be tricky if you don't know the city." Jackson sat down next to Katie. "Coffee?"

"I wish I could stay, but I have a flight to catch." Edward scooped up his phone, glanced at it, and tapped on it a few times before setting it screen-down. "In my haste to get to Albany, I must have left the older pictures of my wife at home. I will have a friend email them to you."

"You could have told us that over the phone," Katie said.

"I honestly thought I had them in my bag, but all I had were these." He pushed the envelope across the table. "These are a few pictures of us from the last couple of years."

Katie pulled the envelope across the table and fiddled with the edges. It wasn't a total waste of time since she had gotten to see Owen and Raif together, but still, she hadn't needed to spend an hour in the car for this.

"I wanted to stay for a few days, hoping you'd find

her quickly, but I'm going to spend some time with friends. I need that right now."

"We understand," Jackson said.

"We'd like to ask you a few more questions." Katie placed her hand on the envelope. "If we're going to have any chance of finding your wife, we need you to tell us everything you can."

"What else do you need to know?"

"Please, don't take offense, but I've been doing this for a long time." Katie paused for a moment, and when Edward didn't protest, she continued. "I am very good at my job and have learned to trust my gut instincts."

"And what does your gut tell you?" Edward folded his hands and leaned across the table.

"That you're not giving us the entire picture," Jackson said.

"You're right." Edward palmed his iPhone again and quickly fiddled with the touchscreen before once again setting it screen-down. "First and foremost, I want my wife back. I love her. I want to tell her that. However, if she no longer wants to be with me after hearing me out, I won't fight her. But I want what she took from me."

Bingo, Katie thought.

"And what did she take?" Jackson asked.

"That's private. Which is why I didn't bring it up."

"Whatever it is, it might help us find her," Katie said.

"Doubtful. I'm paying you a fair amount of money to find my wife. Either you want the job, or you don't."

"We're not saying we don't want the case. However, if this object she took will help make it easier to find her—"

"It won't," Edward said.

"Why do you suppose she took this particular personal item? Is she sending you a message? Is there some other meaning behind the item? Something only the two of you shared?" Katie asked, not wanting to let it go. "Anything you can give us. Even the smallest detail could be the big link we need to locate her for you."

"Ever have something that represents a part of you so personal you couldn't part with it? No matter what? Something you wanted to take to the grave with you?"

"Yes." Katie thumbed her necklace. "This piece of jewelry."

"It's beautiful," Edward said. "If you were to take it off, would it help your partner here find you?"

Katie hated to admit it, but the man had a point. "Not necessarily. Unless it showed up somewhere. If we knew what it was, we could search for it."

Edward stood. "It's not unique or a family heirloom or anything like that. It won't help you find her or even give you any insight into me, her, or our relationship. You have my cell number. I will be in touch in a few days."

Jackson went to stand.

"Don't bother. I'll talk to you soon." Edward turned on his heels and headed toward the door.

"Well, that was interesting," Katie said.

"If I didn't find this so fascinating, I'd say let's dump him as a client. But I want to do more digging, and I'm not doing it for free."

"Works for me." Katie set her sights on Hannah.

"Oh, no, you don't." Jackson waved the waitress over. They both ordered coffee. "The events of this morning are a little too weird, even for us. Adding Hannah to the mix won't be good. Besides, she's been bugging you for that interview."

"That's never going to happen. However, I want to know if she saw Owen and Raif together. If she did, I want to know the spin."

"She's never going to tell you that. And don't look over your shoulder because she's coming this way."

Katie turned, and sure enough, Hannah was standing right behind her, pen and pad in her hands. "Shall we set up an interview time?" Hannah asked.

"Nope," Katie replied.

Hannah put her pen and pad into her purse and then told her crew to wait outside. "How about we talk off the record?"

"Nothing with you is off the record," Katie said.

"How about we exchange some information? I tell you what I saw this afternoon, and you answer a few questions." Hannah stepped to the side of the booth, then dared to sit down next to Jackson, who had the audacity to move over.

"What did you see?" Jackson asked.

"Not until Katie agrees to my terms."

Katie laughed. "I'm not giving you an interview of any kind about anything. You do your thing on your side of the universe, and I'll do mine. There's absolutely no reason for us to mix worlds."

"We can help each other."

"I doubt that," Katie said. "We're not interested in making the evening news."

"Or helping you land your anchor job," Jackson added.

"But you *are* interested in finding the truth about your mother's death and where her body was dumped. I think I can be of some service to you in exchange for an exclusive interview."

"How can you possibly be of service to me? Are you a detective? Do you have some psychic ability where you can communicate with the dead?"

"No need to be sarcastic," Hannah said. "You spy on people. I dig up information and report on what I find. Perhaps I have found some things you might be interested in."

"Like what?" Katie asked, tired of the same song and dance.

"I'm not saying unless we've got a deal."

"Then it's been nice chatting with you," Katie said. "See you around."

"Who was the guy you were just talking with?" Hannah asked, completely ignoring the brush-off.

Katie thought nothing of answering the question

with a complete lie. "My new boyfriend," Katie said. She pulled out her wallet and dumped a five on the table before snagging the envelope. "Let's go." She stood and headed for the door.

"I think you should hear me out," Hannah called.

She turned. "Jackson? Are you coming or what?"

"Yeah," he said but paused to look at Hannah. "I don't think Katie's going to play nice in the sandbox with you now. Or ever. I think you should let it go."

Katie stopped at the door, waiting as she tapped her foot on the floor.

"What about you?" Hannah asked. "Do you play nice?"

"It's not a game. Report the truth, without any spin, and stay out of her way."

"Is that a threat?" Hannah asked.

Jackson shook his head.

"Come on," Katie called. "It's pointless."

"Yeah," Jackson said. "Do you mind?"

Hannah shrugged as she stood, letting Jackson out.

Quickly, Jackson caught up to Katie. "She's smart. I don't get why she doesn't get it."

"Stop trying to understand her. She's not a normal woman."

He pushed the door and held it open. "Neither are you, and I *get* you."

"That's a scary thought. Now, let's get back to work. We've got a missing woman to find."

5

Jacob continued down the path in Washington Park, heading toward the playhouse on the opposite side of the downtown university campus. Bile smacked the back of his throat. He'd been halfway home when the call had come in that a body had been found.

And not just any body.

A female.

About twenty years of age.

With red hair.

Killed by a hunting bow.

There hadn't been a case that could be linked to *The Doe Hunter* in the tri-city area in decades. Hell, he couldn't find one in the state of New York. Why now? Had the Williams girl brought the killer back to the area? Was there some other trigger?

So many unanswered questions, all of which gave him a headache.

"Hey, Jacob. Over here," Cameron said, standing next to a group of police officers.

The forensics team was busy snapping pictures, taking samples, and doing their best to keep the crime scene from being contaminated.

"What do you know?" Jacob asked.

"Not much." Cameron shoved his hands into his pockets. "Her name is Laurie Haley. She was barhopping last night. Her friends wanted to go back to the dorm, but she met some guy."

"Do we have a name?"

"We have a sketch artist working on that with her friends over at the dorms," Cameron said. "But if I can be frank, this doesn't feel like a copycat. It just feels rushed."

"What do you mean?" Jacob glanced around. It appeared that the killer had dragged the body about forty feet so he could hide it in the bushes.

"All the other victims were dehydrated. Bruised. Even sunburned. It was as if they'd been in the elements for a few days. Maybe running from something."

"Hunted," Jacob said. It had been a working theory that *The Doe Hunter* had been hunting his victims for sport as if they were big game. "Any signs of sexual assault?"

"None. And it was a clean shot to the heart. Medical

examiner didn't want to speculate, but he said based on the size of the arrow, he wouldn't be shocked if she died instantly."

"So, she was running through the park, naked, and this asshole hits her with a bow and arrow." Jacob rubbed the back of his neck. "Are there any businesses with security cameras in the area? What about the college?"

"Pulled every one we could. I sent them to the lab, but there isn't a good angle that points to any entrance to the park."

Jacob inched closer the body. It never got easier. It just got different. He swallowed the unsettling feeling that filled his mind and soul as he knelt to examine the wound. "That's one hell of an arrow."

"It's pretty standard," the medical examiner said. "We won't be able to do the autopsy until the morning, but I'll get the report to you as soon as possible."

"Thanks. I appreciate it." Jacob continued studying the young woman whose life had been ripped away way too early. Her long, wavy hair had been pulled over her shoulders, covering her breasts. Her hands had been placed on her genitals, just like all the other girls.

"Cameron, how many different theories are there regarding why this guy stages the scene?"

"Of course, the first is to throw us off. Another is he feels guilt or shame for their nakedness. And the one that I personally find fascinating, is that it's out of respect for the victim."

"That is interesting." Jacob searched his mind but couldn't think of a single girl who'd had short hair. He had half a mind to ask Katie to cut hers off. "I wonder if that's why all his victims have long hair."

"Could very well be," Cameron said.

Jacob stood, wiping his hands on his slacks. "Why the fuck did this guy decide to kill here? Now?"

"Is that a rhetorical question? Or do you want my opinion?" Cameron asked.

"I want to hear your thoughts." Jacob strolled away from the body and the action to where he and Cameron could talk in private.

"My first thought, though I need to study the rest of the cases the Violent Crimes Unit sent over, was that the Williams girl brought him here. But there aren't a lot of places in Albany to go hunting." Jacob rolled his neck. "Do we know where the very first victim that we have a record of in this area was found?"

"You mean besides the Hemming girl, who was found up in the Dix Range?"

"Yes."

"If my memory is correct, there was one in Saratoga that meets the profile, but the crime scene didn't. And she was killed with a regular handgun about six months before the Hemming case."

"He could have been perfecting his signature," Jacob

said. "But there has to be a reason he killed here in this park."

"He could be taunting us."

"If that's the case, he could start to get arrogant and sloppy." While that made Jacob's heart race, he didn't like the idea of any more girls dying at the hands of this asshole. "This guy has been killing for at least twenty-seven years. Let's say he started in his early twenties. That would make him sixty or so. He could be getting too old for the hunt."

"That, too," Cameron said. "But my dad is sixty-three and in the best shape he's ever been in. I think we're looking for a distinguished man who doesn't stand out in a crowd. He cares about his body but doesn't flaunt it because he doesn't like to bring attention to himself. However, he likely doesn't have a lot of friends. At least, not on the surface."

"And he travels a lot," Jacob said. "Not to mention, he leaves the crime scenes virtually clean. All the murder weapons come from all over the country, and it's pretty easy to get a compound bow. Any sporting goods store sells them."

"I'm already to pound the pavement tomorrow and talk to everyone in the tri-state area."

"Good, because I've got that interview tomorrow with the profiler, and I need to go see my dad. He said he's going to show me the files from Owen Bateman's case."

Cameron raised both brows. It was rare that Jacob

ever got a reaction from the kid, so this totally amused him. "Seriously? Because I was going to tell you that before I nearly got caught, I found something interesting."

"Yeah? What was that?"

"There was a set of tire tracks on the street that didn't match Owen's car. But it was thrown out because there was a car down the way with the same tires."

"That's a big piece of information."

"I had to put it away when our agent in charge came into the file room," Cameron said. "Why does the FBI have the entire case file, evidence and all, on this case?"

"Because the money that's missing isn't just from the personal accounts. The foundation was also wiped clean. Technically, it's still an open case. I wouldn't be surprised if someone from this office is keeping tabs on Owen."

"Yeah, but I looked up the address of the car. It wasn't registered to anyone on Rockhurst. It was someone on Cleverdale, pretty far down from the split."

That got Jacob's hackles up.

"And it gets better. It was owned by a little old lady who barely ever drove. She was keeping it to give to her grandson when he graduated from college."

"I assume they did testing on the vehicle," Jacob said.

"I had to close the file before I got that far."

Jacob patted Cameron on the back. "Thanks. I appreciate you doing that for me, but don't risk it again. My old man is going to fill me in. Finally."

"Let me know if I can help."

Jacob nodded. He planted his hands on his hips and stared up at the stars and the moon, searching for answers. They'd seen it all unfold. The sky knew what happened, but it couldn't tell Jacob anything. "I want a copy of the sketch of the last man seen with the victim."

"I'll wait around until everything is wrapped up."

"Are you sure you don't mind?" Jacob asked.

"No. I live twenty minutes from here. You're an hour away. I'll call you if anything happens."

Jacob turned and headed toward the entrance as he pulled out his cell. First call, his dad.

It rang once.

"I saw it on the news," his dad said.

Of course, his father wouldn't even start with a hello. "I'm just leaving the scene now. I'm not going to make it tonight. I need to go home and talk with Katie."

"It scares both your mother and me that both the Williams girl and this last victim have red hair. Like Katie."

"I know, Dad. It freaks me out, too."

"Grace had red hair," his father said softly.

Jacob paused, dead in his tracks. That was not something he'd ever entertained. "Are you suggesting that my killer murdered Katie's mom?" He'd never mentioned the cold cases to his old man. He couldn't.

But that didn't mean his father didn't know about them. "Because that would be a very long time for a killer to be inactive, and we both know the only way that happens is if they're incarcerated." Jacob knew baiting his father that way would cause a fight, but he wanted to know what he knew, and sometimes asking him point-blank didn't work.

"You're joking, right?"

"Not until you put it in my head."

His father let out a short laugh. "You forget, I have friends in high places, and I know there are more cases than those two girls that span many years and a dozen states."

Jacob opened the driver's side of his beat-up old clunker. He honestly couldn't wait until he picked up his new pickup. But he wasn't getting his damn muffler fixed. No point in putting money into a piece of shit. "So, why are you suggesting that Grace could be one of my killer's victims?"

"I'm not. I'm making an observation."

A good one, but Jacob wasn't about to give that credit to his father just yet.

"When did you come up with this little idea? While you were sitting in Owen's car in downtown Albany?"

"I guess you saw the news."

"No. Someone from the office saw you. And so did Katie," Jacob admitted. "What did the news report say? I haven't had the chance to talk with Katie."

"Hannah's a real fucking piece of work."

"Tell me something I don't know." Jacob turned the engine over and pulled out into traffic.

"I don't know what you ever saw in her."

"We all make mistakes, Dad. Can we please focus on her news report?"

"Sure," his father said. "Basically, she wondered why I would meet an ex-client in a parking lot and not at my office. She then implied that maybe it had to do with the missing money and commented on my financial status."

Jacob smacked the steering wheel. He knew Hannah to be ruthless, but that was below the belt. "That's low, even for her. But no offense, it does look odd that you met him there."

"It wasn't planned."

"What do you mean?" Jacob eased onto the thruway. He couldn't get home fast enough. All he wanted to do was steal a few kisses. Maybe get a chance to cuddle, and hopefully, continue to heal old wounds.

"My receptionist left me a message that Owen called, asking to meet me."

"Doesn't he have a cell phone?"

"He does. I was told it died and that he really needed me, so I went running," his father said. "Owen, in turn, got a call, supposedly from someone in my office, stating that I was in Albany working a case and that I needed to see him. That it was important."

"Do you have that number?"

"I do. A friend already ran it. It's bogus. One of those made-up things you can do on a cell."

"I still want it," Jacob said.

"Fine, I'll text it to you."

"Dad. You should have come to me with all of this sooner."

"I know that now, son. But that's all in the past. Let's just keep moving forward," his father said. "And don't forget, your mom will be doing her annual celebration of life for your brother."

Jacob sucked in a deep breath. It was more like paying homage to the son she wished had survived. Deep down, Jacob knew that if the tables were turned, and he had died in that fire, Jonathon would have been feeling the same way he did. But that wasn't the case.

"Is there anything you need me to do?" Jacob asked.

"Just the same thing you do every year. Be understanding. I know this is hard on you, but you hold your mom at arm's length just as much as you say she does to you."

Tears stung Jacob's eyes. It wasn't love that he lacked. It was affection. Warmth. The undying fondness a mother has for her son. His mother had tried. She'd tucked him in every night. Read to him. She'd kissed his boo-boos like every other mother. But Jacob had always felt as though something was missing. He'd see the bonds other little boys had with their mothers, and he just didn't have that with his.

All of that had been buried with Jonathon.

Katie tossed the pictures of MaryAnn onto the coffee table and stretched out on the sofa, flipping through the channels, trying not to stare at the clock, which currently blinked ten in the evening. She also tried to avoid the channel that Hannah worked for.

She'd had enough of that bitch for one day.

Between her run-in at the dinner and what she'd implied about Jacob's dad, well, Katie wouldn't mind giving Hannah a piece of her mind.

Raif Donovan might have defended her uncle, but he wasn't a criminal.

And the fact that Jacob's mom had corroborated Raif's story about the fact that he'd never had an affair with her mother, well, Katie had to wonder where the fuck Hannah had gotten her information.

She had half a mind to call the woman up and ask her.

But Jacob would never forgive her, and they were finally on really good terms.

Maybe too good.

She touched her lips. She'd missed Jacob these past years. Granted, she'd been living with him for the last year, but that didn't really count since they'd barely spoken to one another until recently.

Four years ago, when she'd broken up with Jacob, she'd made the biggest mistake of her life. He'd been working at the district attorney's office, which had been his dream job. All he ever talked about was being on the other side of the courtroom as his father. But then the shit had hit the fan, and Katie ruined everything.

When Jackson had gotten together with his wife, Shannon, Katie finally realized how badly she'd screwed up, but by then, it was too late. Jacob had already slept with Hannah.

Of course, that'd lasted only a month or two. But then he quit his job, went to Quantico, and became an FBI agent, creating more distance.

Becoming a federal agent wasn't a bad fit for Jacob, and he was really good at his new career, but it wasn't his passion. Not even close. And it showed.

The hum of the garage door opening made her jump. She nearly spilled her double shot of whiskey on the rocks, which was more than watered down at this point. She swung her legs to the floor but didn't stand. She didn't want to appear too eager to see Jacob, which was stupid. He knew that she was waiting up for him so they could discuss everything that had transpired today and exchange notes.

"Honey, I'm home." Jacob closed and locked the door as he tossed his backpack and sport coat onto the chair in the family room.

She smiled. "That's really getting old."

"Then why do you have a huge grin?" He disappeared into the kitchen.

She heard a cabinet opening and closing and then clattering ice cubes.

"Because you're going to get me a refill with ice."

"Your wish is my command." He rounded the corner, holding two fresh glasses. He handed her one and took a seat on the other end of the sofa. He took a generous sip as he set his feet on the table. "Those woman's eyes really freak me out."

"Tell me about it," Katie said.

"Did you get pictures of her from when she was a kid?"

Katie shook her head. "Edward didn't bring them with him. Said he'd have someone email them to us tomorrow. I'm not holding my breath."

Jacob's feet hit the floor with a thud. He leaned forward and lifted one of the photos, raising it as if the overhead light would bring some kind of clarity to the picture. "It looks like she's had some plastic surgery."

"Jackson's contacting surgeons in Vegas to see if anyone knows her. Hopefully, he'll get a hit."

"Why don't you believe Edward will get you pictures from her childhood?" Jacob set the photograph down and lifted Katie's feet, setting them on his lap. He always gave the best foot rubs, and right now, his hands were pure magic.

She should pull away because the more she let him touch her, the more likely she was to do something she might regret. She wasn't ready to completely let go of all the pains of the past. The lies of his family and his personal betrayal still squeezed at her heart.

But at the same time, during the last year, his presence made her feel safe. Something she hadn't felt since her uncle had been released.

"Because he's avoided it from the get-go." Katie let herself relax, something she hadn't really done in a long time. "If she was from this area but hasn't been here in years, it doesn't take a private eye to think a photo from her childhood might be able to pinpoint where she might have gone, especially if she lied about her real name." She held up her hand. "And today, his demeanor wasn't a husband concerned for his wife's safety but rather a man who wanted a possession back. And that wasn't a person, but an actual thing."

"What do you mean?"

"He said she took something from him and that he wanted it back."

Jacob stopped rubbing her feet for a brief moment. "More than he wants his wife?"

"He said that if she wanted to leave him, so be it, but that he still wanted what she took. However, he wouldn't tell us what that was."

"Something's not right with this guy." Jacob went back to working out the soreness in her soles.

"Jackson's taking the lead. He says I'm all over the place between her haunting eyes and Owen."

"I've got an idea." Jacob snagged his drink and took a sip before shifting her body and lowering himself behind her, tucking her against his chest as he wrapped his strong arms around her in an intimate embrace.

Part of her wished she'd do what she'd done a few months ago and push off any kind of advance he made. But the truth was, it felt too good.

"I'm listening," she said.

"Let me take this photograph to our lab and have them run diagnostics on it. They can do an age regression and get an idea of what she might have looked like years ago."

"Even though she's had a bit of plastic surgery?"

"They can do their best." He tugged at her ponytail holder, setting her long hair free. He brushed it to the side before pressing his warm, soft lips against her neck just under her ear. His hand rubbed up and down her arm.

She resisted the urge to twist her body and face him. That would only lead to heavy petting and most likely an invitation to her bed. That wasn't a good idea.

"Okay. You can take one." She took his hand, bringing it to her cheek and using it as a pillow. Closing her eyes, she inhaled sharply.

"Can I have a picture of Edward?"

"Sure," she said. "Just because we're lying here together doesn't mean I totally forgive you or that I'm ready for anything to happen."

"That's an indication that you might be ready someday."

"You're like a dog with a bone." She blinked. "I know that what I said when we broke up hurt you."

"Hearing that my dad slept with your mom was a shocker."

"It wasn't just that. It was that Raif didn't deny it. He didn't comment, and neither did your mother, which I took as it being the truth. I was so angry, and I thought maybe you had known. You've always been so close to your dad."

"I can understand that, but you wouldn't listen to me. You never gave me a chance. However, what I did next has to be the biggest mistake of my life, and I will regret it forever."

Needing to look into his eyes, she shifted. She caught his gaze, staring deep into his soft, sensitive orbs. She'd always been able to tell what he was feeling by what she saw in those ice-blue eyes, and right now all she saw was love and admiration with a tinge of remorse.

"I'm truly sorry," he whispered.

"So am I." She caved to her desire. The kiss was like an old dance set to new music. It was familiar but had all the excitement of being with him for the very first time. It was slow and tender and had all the promise of love and passion.

Until his pocket vibrated.

They both jumped.

"Shit. Sorry." He reached between them and pulled out his cell. "It's my partner. I've got to take this." He pushed himself to a sitting position. "Hey, Cameron. What's up?"

Katie wished she could hear the other side of the conversation, but Jacob kept the phone to his ear. She set her feet on the floor and found her whiskey, downing half of it in one gulp. It burned her throat, reminding her that she wasn't ready to let Jacob all the way in. Not yet.

There was still too much hurt and still too many unanswered questions when it came to Raif and her mother. She needed the truth. Of course, Jacob had nothing to do with any of that, but still, she couldn't manage to completely separate him from the family.

"You've got to be fucking kidding me," Jacob said, glancing at his watch. "I can be there in a half-hour. What about you?"

Jacob nodded. "All right. Why don't you stay put? By the time you get all the way up here, they will probably be done with the crime scene. I'll call you in the morning." Jacob set his phone on his lap. "I've got another body."

"The same killer as the Williams girl and tonight in Washington Park?"

"It appears so, but there's a twist." He rubbed his temples. "She was found on Turtle Island, of all places. The scene was staged, and the man she was camping with was found with a bullet to his brain in the bow of their boat."

Katie gasped. "There are pictures of my mom, me, and my uncle on Turtle Island when I was a little girl."

Jacob arched a brow. "Do you still have them?"

She cocked her head. "Of course, I do."

"Get them out for me. I want to see them when I get back." He leaned in and kissed her. Hard. "I have no idea how long I'll be, so don't wait up. Just either leave them on my bed or on the kitchen table."

"I have a really bad feeling in the pit of my gut," Katie said. "There are no coincidences."

Jacob stood. "I also want everything you and Jackson have on your client."

"You really think he's your killer?"

"I don't know that it adds up." Jacob shrugged. "But he comes to town, and suddenly I've got two dead bodies? That's something I need to look at. Not to mention his missing wife. That's just way too suspicious for me."

"I'll get all the files for you."

"Thanks."

She stood and walked him to the door. "Be safe out there, okay?"

He took her chin with his thumb and forefinger. "Always." He kissed her softly. "Lock up behind me."

She waited until he got into his boat and pulled out of the slip.

Too many things didn't add up, and everything collided. Never a good sign.

6

Jacob tied his boat up next to the Lake George Patrol and flashed his badge. "I'm Special Agent Jacob Donovan."

"I've heard about you," the state trooper said. "You're friends with Stacey Sutton, aren't you?"

"We went to high school together." Jacob stepped onto the dock. "Is she here?"

"Stacey was first on the scene," the trooper said. "She's up there with our boss."

"Jared Blake is here, too?" Jared had been a local trooper for as long as Jacob could remember.

And he was one of the best. His team was loyal and rarely left, except to raise their families or when retirement came their way.

"He was camping with his family a few islands away," the trooper said. "He's on the boat where the male victim was found." The trooper pointed to a thirty-foot cabin cuddy.

"Thanks." Jacob sidestepped the trooper and got Jared's attention. "Long time no see," he said.

"I heard you were on your way here." Jared offered him a hand as he hurled his leg over the side of the boat. "Our victim is Jeff Radish. He's twenty-six, and our killer shot three times. Once in the head, twice in the heart."

"That sounds like overkill, no pun intended." Jacob bent over to get a look at the scene. "Based on the blood pattern, the body had to have been dragged here."

"The neighbors said the boat was gone for most of the day, and the ones to the immediate right didn't see it when they went to bed. My guess is that none of this happened here."

"Who found the bodies and when?" Jacob stood and adjusted his weapon as he scanned the area. Everyone on the island that he could see was sitting on their docks or at picnic benches, huddled together, watching and waiting.

"Sadly, a bunch of kids from the camp over on Pilot Knob are on the other side of the island. The counselor and aide were sneaking away for a couple of beers and found the girl. Stacey found the male victim when she got here."

"That sucks," Jacob mumbled. "What are your thoughts?"

"Well, other than the boyfriend being a complication, I'd say this is *The Doe Killer*. But that's your expertise, not mine."

"Do you mind if your forensic teams send all the evidence to my labs?"

"You don't even have to ask. You've got my full cooperation on this," Jared said.

"Thanks. I'd better go check out the other body." Jacob headed up the path toward the flashing lights of the forensic team.

Bile bubbled from his gut to his throat. His first partner had told him that it was time to quit if he ever got used to murder scenes.

"Jacob." Stacey waved.

"Well, if it isn't Watson," Jacob said with a slight chuckle.

"Don't you think that's getting a little old?"

"Never," he said. "I wish I could say it was good to see you." He squeezed her arm. "I ran into Doug a few weeks ago, and he said you two were expecting. But, wow. You're really showing."

"Yeah. I'm about five months now." She patted her belly. "When are you going to talk Katie into letting Doug and my dad renovate her place?"

"As soon as she has the money."

"I wish there hadn't been a lean on it. Doug would have bought it in a heartbeat." She pressed her hands to the center of her lower back. "I never did understand why she couldn't sell."

"It has to do with the foundation and the missing money. Technically, she doesn't own it but has use of it because of who she is. So, last year, she decided to move in."

"And you couldn't let her do that by herself."

"No, I couldn't," he said. "But that's obviously not why I'm here." He nodded toward the naked female body propped up in the fireplace. Her long, red hair covered her breasts, and her hands covered her private parts as if she were modest about her body. She had an arrow through the center of her chest. "I wasn't given the name on my way up."

"Jessica Downs. Twenty-two. She and her boyfriend took a week off and came to the area." Stacey pointed to her hands. "She has an engagement ring, which her family said is new as of this trip. Her father said he only knew about it because her boyfriend asked for her hand."

"That really sucks," Jacob muttered. "What else can you tell me?"

"Other than they weren't killed here? Not much," Stacey said. "We'll have extra troopers on the lake tomorrow, searching for clues and to interview people. We do have one lead, though."

"And what's that?"

"The people next door said they saw the boat docked at the Black Mountain picnic area around noon."

Jacob ran a hand across his longer-than-normal

hair. "My guy likes to hunt his victims as if they're prey."

"Black Mountain would be a great place for that."

"But he normally takes his time. Like days."

"Maybe he was in a hurry, or she gave up, or her boyfriend got in the way," Stacey said, stating exactly what Jacob had been thinking, circling him right back to Katie's client, who'd left town in a rush.

Or did he?

Jacob made a mental note to make sure to check all the flights out of the Albany airport.

"I sent a text to my partner. Our team is en route, so you don't have to clean up this mess or deal with transport. I appreciate everything you and Jared and the rest of your team has done."

"Anything for you." She patted his shoulder. "Make sure you tell Katie I said hi. Doug and I would love to have you both over for dinner."

"We're not a couple."

"You should be," Stacey said.

"Tell that to Katie." He stuffed his hands into his pockets. "Then again, how long did it take you and Doug to figure things out?"

Stacey cocked her head. "That's way different, and you know it."

"Maybe so." Jacob smiled. "I'll talk to you soon." He strolled down to the docks and hopped into his boat. A slight breeze kicked up. It had been an unseasonably cool June, and he wished he'd at least remembered to bring his sport coat. He turned the key and hit both the starboard and port engine start buttons. It would take him twenty minutes to get home.

He glanced at his watch.

One in the morning.

At least he might get a few hours of sleep.

His phone vibrated. Again. He pulled his cell from his back pocket. Katie had texted him at least four times. He hadn't responded because he hadn't had much to report.

And he wanted to talk this out in person.

Katie: *I can't sleep.*

Jacob: *Go to bed. I'm on my way home, and I'm dead-dog tired. We'll talk in the morning.*

Katie: *Is it The Doe Hunter?*

Katie just never quit.

Jacob: *I believe so. And I can't shake the feeling that your client is somehow involved in all of this. Let's have breakfast at six. We'll chat before I go to my dad's. Now get some sleep. You need it. I'll be home in ten.*

Katie: *Okay. Goodnight.*

He continued to navigate his way through the open waters of Lake George with not another boat in sight. By the time he docked at the Bateman estate, it was one-fifteen, and all he wanted to do was get the grime off his body. He secured his boat and made his way toward the house. It used to look so modern and hip from the water when he'd been a little boy.

Now, it looked as if it could be in a horror movie. And he chose to call it home.

If he went in through the garage, he'd wake Katie for sure, so he opted to use his key at the front door. Fortunately, the new one didn't squeak. He knew she wasn't asleep yet, but he tiptoed up the stairs anyway. Thankfully, her door was closed.

He slipped into his room and tossed his clothes onto the bed. The sooner he showered, the sooner he'd be asleep.

The pipes rattled as he waited for the hot water to kick in. He stepped into the shower and closed his eyes as the steam filled the room. The sound of the shower door opening caught his attention. He blinked. "Katie. What the hell are you doing?"

She wrapped her arms around him and pressed her naked body against his. "Hopefully, something I won't regret in the morning."

"It is the morning." He cupped her cheeks as the water dampened her red hair. "And if there is any chance that being with me is something you don't want, then I don't want it, either."

Her hands glided up and down his back. "I know I want it. I'm just not sure I can commit to it."

He let out a short chuckle. You're naked in my shower. That's being committed to something."

She tilted her head. "You know what I mean."

He brushed his lips over hers, letting them linger

until he couldn't stand it any longer. He pulled back, blinking. "I still lo—"

"Don't say it." She kissed his neck.

"Why not? It's true."

"Do you remember the first time we met as adults?"

He smiled. "Like it was yesterday. I couldn't believe you even gave me the time of day, considering who my old man was."

"I almost didn't, but you charmed the pants right off me. Literally. I was an eighteen-year-old freshman, and you were a twenty-one-year-old junior. And every girl wanted you."

"Not true. Besides, I only had eyes for you." He shut off the water and snagged a couple of towels, wrapping their bodies in them. "I fell in love with you the moment I saw you."

She wrung out her hair and padded into the bedroom, planting her butt on the side of the mattress. Thankfully, still wrapped in a towel, though he knew that wouldn't last long as it appeared she had no plans of going anywhere anytime soon, and there was no way he could resist her. Not anymore.

He wasn't even going to try.

If she broke his heart, he'd deal with it.

But he wouldn't break hers. Not ever again. If he was going to be with her, it would be only her. Forever. She might not be able to commit all the way, but he could. He would never hurt her again.

"Hannah wanted you, even back then."

"Jesus. Why are you bringing her up now?" He adjusted his towel before raking a hand across his wet head.

"I know. She's a mood killer, but I need to know something." She patted her hand on the bed.

He couldn't deny Katie anything, so he joined her. "What's that?"

"During the short time you dated her after she broke the story—that now appears to be a lie—she told me that you and she had a thing in college."

"And you believed her?"

"No," Katie said flatly. "Okay. Maybe a little."

"You do not wear jealousy well." He tucked a piece of hair behind her ear.

"I wouldn't call it that, exactly. But what you did hurt, and she enjoyed rubbing it in every chance she got. Hell, she still does."

He nodded. He'd seen that firsthand, and he'd once tried to put a stop to it. Unfortunately, all that did was add fuel to the fire because Hannah then told Katie that he and Hannah had gone out and had a picture to prove it. He had no idea who'd snapped the photo, but it was staged and not at all an accurate representation of the conversation they'd had.

"The only other girl I dated in college was Sally," he said.

"I actually liked her."

"Yeah. She was nice. But not my type," he admitted.

"Other than to tell Hannah to go fuck herself, I didn't speak to her or have anything to do with her at all. I think she's a snake and a low-life reporter who would toss her own mother under the bus to get ahead."

"Maybe we should give her something to talk about?"

He jerked his head back. "That's like pouring gas on a forest fire."

Katie laughed. "Perhaps. But she's poking around anyway. What if we use her to our advantage?"

"I don't like that idea. The last thing I need is public panic, and that's exactly what Hannah will invoke."

"I can guarantee that by tomorrow morning's news, she will have already linked the cases. She might be a bitch, but she's not stupid."

"What are you proposing?"

"That I give her that interview she's been begging for. That will get her off the murder cases, at least for a bit, and focus her attention on my uncle again. And maybe she can help us connect the dots to my client."

"That's actually brilliant."

She stood and gave him a good shove in the center of his chest and then straddled him.

He groaned. "But are you sure you want to put yourself through the kinds of questions that Hannah is going to ask you?"

"Well, perhaps I need to have a chat with your father and my uncle."

He arched a brow. "Only if I'm present."

"Deal." She tossed her towel across the room. "So. Are you going to kick me out?"

"Hell, no."

Katie couldn't believe that she was back in Jacob's arms or how good it felt.

Better than she remembered.

He'd always been a tender lover. Gentle and kind. But at the same time, he could be aggressive. While he'd had a lover or two before her, he'd been Katie's first, and he'd taught her what true passion was all about. The few men she'd been with since paled in comparison.

She tried not to use Jacob as a benchmark, but it was impossible.

And right now, she remembered why as he gently lay her on her back and kissed his way down her taut belly. His hands massaged her breasts as his thumbs rubbed across her hard nipples.

Arching her back, she moaned.

He nestled his head between her legs. When they first started dating, he'd always told her that he cared more about her orgasm than his, and he'd proven that point time and again, making sure she had one, oftentimes forgoing his pleasure entirely, especially in the beginning.

But that didn't last long as Katie quickly grew into her sexuality. She wanted to please him as much as he did her, and it often became a battle of wills.

However, that wasn't the case now. She would enjoy being back in his bed because she didn't know if she would allow herself the simple pleasure again. It wasn't that she didn't love Jacob, but that she did with all her heart. She'd never stopped. But her damned ego got in the way.

He pinched and twisted her nipples as his tongue danced across her hard nub like a soft feather floating in the wind. It was a kind of magical torture that made a person beg, but when it happened, only made them wish it could last forever.

She dug her heels into the bed, and her toes curled. She was desperate to maintain control. He knew her body, and he played it like a fiddle.

Blinking, she glanced down, which was a mistake. She gasped, clutching his head. It always amazed her that all he ever needed was his tongue. She held her breath, trying to hold off for as long as she could, but it was a losing battle.

He opened his eyes, and they locked gazes.

Her climax ripped through her gut, making her shake uncontrollably. She tugged at his hair but he didn't stop. At least not for a good minute as her body continued to convulse. Her muscles contracted.

"Jacob," she managed.

He lifted his head and made his way up to her lips, kissing them softly. "Yes," he said with a wicked grin.

She cupped his cheeks. "You're awfully proud of yourself."

"I'll be more so when I make it happen again."

"You'd better, but not until I reacquaint myself with your body."

He groaned, rolling to his back. "I learned a long time ago not to argue with you."

"Yeah, right." She inhaled sharply as she shamelessly stared.

"Go easy on me. It's been a while."

"What's *a while?*" She splayed her hand over the center of his chest, gently digging her nails into his skin as she dragged them across his nipples.

He hissed. "Before I moved into this house."

She arched a brow. "More than a year?"

"That surprises you?"

"It does," she admitted.

"And what about you?"

She leaned over and pressed her lips to his tight abs. "I plead the fifth." Before he could comment, she took him into her hands and teased, gently stroking and squeezing. This had always been one of her favorite parts of being with Jacob.

Not so much with anyone else.

She never understood why, and she never tried to analyze it.

This had been something she'd held as sacred; part

of the lovemaking she shared with the only man she'd ever loved.

As she brought him to her lips, she realized she didn't think she could ever love another man the way she loved Jacob. They had a connection that was so unique, so special, that even when they weren't together, they were still drawn to one another.

Soul mates.

He threaded his hands through her hair, piling it on the top of her head. His body tensed and relaxed depending on the pressure she applied. His breathing got labored, and a few deep moans escaped his lips.

"Katie," he whispered. "Time to stop."

It was always bittersweet when the teasing had to end, but her skin tingled in anticipation of what was about to happen.

She climbed on top of him, positioning herself to accept his length.

He arched, thrusting into her as if he couldn't wait.

And, honestly, neither could she. A sense of desperation washed over her. It was as if she didn't feel release now, she might never. But she knew that wasn't true. She tried to keep things slow. Controlled. Almost rhythmic.

However, it appeared that even Jacob struggled with that as he gripped her hips and flipped her onto her back. He kissed her hard. It was wet and sloppy, and she wouldn't have had it any other way.

She wrapped her legs around his powerful body and let go. Every muscle shaking with her climax.

He arched his back and held still for a long moment, letting his own release overtake him as it collided with hers in the perfect storm. He stared down at her, and she locked gazes with his intense ice-blue eyes. He held her captive, but she was fine with that. She didn't mind being his. Because deep down, she wanted to believe that he was hers.

"Katie," he whispered. "I do love you."

She blinked. She desperately wanted to accept his love and be able to give it back. Because she felt it. She truly did.

She opened her mouth, but before she could even let out a grunt, he brushed his lips over hers.

"You don't need to say it back. I know you're not ready." He snuggled next to her, pulling the covers over their bodies.

"It's not that I don't." She rested her head on his chest.

"I know that." He kissed her temple. "You and me, we've been through a lot. Maybe I shouldn't have said it so soon, but I'm the one who has the redeeming to do, and I plan on letting you know every day just how important you are to me."

"That might be fun."

He chuckled. "Let's get some sleep. I've got to get up at the crack of dawn."

"Jacob?" She tilted her head.

"Yes?"

"Thank you."

"For what?"

"For understanding me." She closed her eyes, and for the first time in a long while, she drifted off to sleep feeling as though things might be looking up.

7

Jacob shifted on the leather sofa in the waiting room of his father's office, flipping through some star-filled magazine. He'd planned on stopping by first thing, but he'd had a shit ton of paperwork to deal with and a few interviews.

The case had to come first.

Though, Katie had been hounding him about her idea to let Hannah interview her. More importantly, her desire to, all of a sudden, get together with her uncle and his father.

Something Jacob desperately didn't think she should do alone.

He tapped his foot on the floor. Sometimes, it peeved him that his dad could keep him waiting. Especially knowing how important this was. And second, that it was still business hours and Jacob was on the clock.

His father's law practice took up two floors and had been decorated by his mother's delicate hand and impeccable tastes. His parents had always been into the finer things. If it wasn't top quality, what was the point? Jacob would try to argue that sometimes practicality trumped quality, and the only time his father agreed was with cars. But still, his dad drove a Lexus, a vehicle of status.

Jacob understood why his mother did it. She poured her emotions into things instead of her one living son. But he wasn't sure why his father did. Perhaps it was just to keep the peace with his mom.

"Jacob," Ms. Beatle said. "Your father is free now."

"Thanks." He smiled, stood, and made his way across the waiting area. He eyed the funky container sitting on the corner of her desk, just like he had over twenty years ago.

"Go ahead," she said. "I still carry your favorite."

Quickly, he reached his hand across the desk, opened the lid, and scooped out a handful of miniature chocolates. "How come you never put anything else in the jar?"

"I'm always hoping you'll come to visit your father." She stood to escort him down the long twisty halls of Donovan, Hillard, and Tate.

"Not necessary. I don't get lost here anymore."

"All right," she said. "Enjoy your visit."

Jacob chewed on a piece of chocolate while stuffing a few more into his coat pocket. When he was a kid, the idea was to finish the candy before he found his way to his father's office. Pretty much the only reason he used to get lost. Of course, he was eating at least three pieces at a time back then.

He bumped into a few lawyers he'd seen in court, and a few others who had known him when he was in diapers—they enjoyed letting him know that. He had spent a lot of time in this office. His fondest memories were when Katie joined him. They'd always get into some good debates regarding criminal law and which side of the fence was better. He and Katie had always gone for putting the criminals away, while his dad and partners would cross-examine them with the finer points of how the system really worked.

Jacob tapped on his father's half-open office door.

"Come on in." His father was behind his big maple desk, seated in his tufted leather chair. He leaned back with his feet up on his desk while tossing a little basketball up into the air. That ball was the only thing he'd kept that had belonged to Jonathon, Jacob's brother. "I heard you had another murder."

"This case is getting weirder and weirder. Not to mention broader and possibly spanning decades."

"So you've mentioned."

Jacob sat down in one of the comfortable chairs his mother had carefully picked out. Everything, like at home, matched perfectly. "We've got a lot I want to cover, and I don't have a ton of time."

"What do you want to start with?" Jacob glanced above his father to the family photo taken when Jacob had graduated from college.

Katie had taken the picture. It had been one of the happiest days in Jacob's life. He would continue at Albany Law School, and Katie would continue her undergrad. Life would remain the same.

At least, for a few years.

"How many times did Grace disappear before she did for good?"

"She was a wild child," his father said. "She left home for the first time when she was eighteen, as I recall. I was away at college, so I don't rightly remember too much. But Owen was so distraught over it, he left school for a couple of weeks."

"Where did she go?"

"I actually don't know." His father leaned forward. "Why do you want to know about this part of Grace's past?"

"A lot of reasons, one of which I'll get to shortly."

"You sound like a lawyer."

"That's because I am," Jacob said with a short laugh. He'd only been an active FBI agent for a year and a half. And while he enjoyed his job, he missed the courtroom. "Do you think Owen has any idea who Katie's father is?"

"He begged Grace to tell him when she returned

home with a one-year-old, but she wouldn't. When Katie was two, Grace disappeared for about three weeks."

"Did she take Katie?" Jacob asked.

His father shook his head. "By then, Owen knew for sure that Grace was bipolar. When she was on her meds, she was fine. But off them, not so much."

"Katie remembers her mother having an enormous amount of energy and always smiling."

"She was manic a lot. Your mother tried to help by befriending Grace and—"

Jacob held up his hand. "I have to know why Mom didn't defend you and stop the rumor about the affair."

"For one, your mom felt that if either of us commented or denied, it would perpetuate the lie. I'm inclined to agree with her since the story died pretty quickly."

"People still whisper about it."

"Perhaps. But Hannah found no proof. She came up emptyhanded and all but made a fool of herself when she couldn't find any real evidence of this alleged affair. A good reporter doesn't report on something that isn't a fact."

"That is true," Jacob said.

"And, secondly, your mother hates Hannah. I mean, she can't stand that woman. I once had the news on that channel and she took off her shoes, tossed them at the television, and swore like a drunken sailor."

Jacob smiled. "I would have loved to see Mom do that."

"It did warm my heart just a little, but that story wasn't the first time Hannah came poking around this family."

"Excuse me?" Jacob gripped the sides of the chair. "What does that mean?"

"About a year after that, she came asking about how the fire that killed your brother got started."

Jacob's heart dropped to the pit of his stomach. Hannah had asked him about that a few times, but she'd masked it as her being a concerned girlfriend.

However, Jacob never discussed it with anyone except his old man.

And Katie.

"Why didn't you tell me? I would have dumped that bitch long before I did."

"Why did you go out with her in the first place?" his father asked. "That's something your mother and I have never been able to figure out."

"I guess you could call it a case of self-loathing."

That made his father chuckle, though there was nothing funny about it.

"Okay. So. You never had an affair with Grace. But what makes you so sure that Owen didn't kill her?"

His father pointed to five large boxes. "Everything I have on Owen's case is in those."

"Do I get to take them?"

"They can't leave this office, but you can have a key

and the security codes. I've already gotten approval from the partners."

"And Katie?"

To Jacob's surprise, his father nodded.

"On my own, I've learned about a partial print, tire tracks that weren't Owen's but were thrown out for bogus reasons, and you told me about the five hundred thousand dollars before she disappeared."

"Wow. I'm impressed. Dare I ask how you dug up the rest? It's not in any public record."

"I'm good at my job, Dad." Jacob rose and sauntered over to the boxes. He lifted one of the lids. The folders inside were meticulous and neatly marked. As if he'd expected anything different.

"I have no doubt." His father joined him in front of the boxes. He shoved his hands into his pockets. "I have gone over everything in those boxes numerous times, and I can't find the smoking gun. But, to be honest, Owen hasn't given me much to go on, either. He's adamant that by him going to jail, he saved Katie's life."

"Do you think he's keeping something from you?"

"I hate to admit it, but I do. When I met with him the other day in the parking lot of the diner, he made me promise that I'd call you in. I told him I'd already done that."

"Why me?"

"Because you're my son. And because he's seen you with Katie. He believes you'll protect her at all costs."

"Well, he's got that right."

"Jacob. That meeting was a setup, and it's got Owen spooked. Bad. He's terrified that someone is going to kill Katie."

"And he won't tell you who?" Jacob stared at his father. "He's got to have some idea."

"He says he can't trust his memory because whoever killed Grace drugged him. They found the date rape drug in his system, along with a bunch of alcohol. I found that disturbing and odd."

"Why would he take that?" Jacob asked. "It doesn't make sense."

"I've questioned that a million times, but the prosecution managed to use it to show Owen as a man out of his mind," his father said.

"Does he remember anything from that night?"

"He thinks he heard Grace call out the name *Thurston*, but he can't be sure. He also thinks he might be able to recall some features about the man, but he doesn't trust his memory."

"I can get a sketch artist."

"I think he'd be down for that," his father said.

"Do you think he'd be down for having a chat with me and Katie?"

His father jerked his head back. "She wants that?"

Jacob nodded. "But neither of you might like what she wants to do."

"And what's that?"

"She wants to let Hannah interview her."

His dad raked a hand over his head. "That is a bad fucking idea. That woman is heartless."

"Not to mention ruthless, and she'll do anything for a byline. However, I think Katie's right. We can use Hannah to our advantage."

"You can't control a woman like that, son."

"Maybe we don't want to control her. Maybe we want to use her to bring a killer to the surface and find out once and for all what happened to Grace Bateman."

"What the fuck is going on?" Katie stood in the middle of her family room and stared at a picture of her mother. It was one she'd never seen before. "How the hell did that get here?"

"Hell if I know," Jackson said. "Cops are on their way. So is Jacob. He said that he was ten minutes out."

"Thanks." She leaned over to get a better look at the image. She guessed her mother to be about the same age as she had been when she died, but it had to have been taken before that because her hair was lighter. More a strawberry blond than light red.

But had her hair ever been lighter?

Katie's hair had been lighter as a kid, but as she'd grown into adulthood, it'd become more of a dark red.

She'd have to go pull out the family albums. They'd be able to tell her when this picture had been taken.

"Someone is fucking with me. A week ago, I would

have totally believed that it was my uncle Owen."

"We're still tailing him, and he's been at work all day. Just to be sure, I've got someone checking with his supervisor."

"Thanks. But this doesn't feel like something he'd do."

"You don't even know him. Why do you say that?"

"Because he's left me alone since the day he went to prison. The only time he's come near me was the other day, and that was to warn me. So why now, all of a sudden? It's not the anniversary of anything. It's not my birthday. Or his. It doesn't make sense."

"I agree. I just wanted to know what you were thinking." Jackson squeezed her shoulder. "By the way, I never got an email from Edward and—"

"Jacob had an interesting idea."

"He always does."

"Edward showed up, and suddenly Jacob's got two dead girls."

Jackson tilted his head. "And your house was broken into. And let's not state the obvious..." He reached out and touched her hair. "Not to mention, he never boarded any plane at the Albany airport."

She shivered. "Jacob was going to look into when and where *The Doe Hunter* might have gotten his start. What if he killed my mother?"

"Then I'd say you need twenty-four-hour protection, and Owen knows more than he's letting on."

"Makes me wonder what Raif isn't telling us."

The sound of footsteps racing through the house caught her attention. She glanced over.

"Katie. Are you okay?" Jacob practically shoved Jackson out of the way and yanked her to his chest.

"I'm fine, only you're crushing me."

He cupped her face and gingerly kissed her lips.

"Shucks, man," Jackson said. "Don't I get one of those?"

"Maybe next time." Jacob bent over and glanced at the picture. "You've really never seen it before?"

"Nope," she said.

The doorbell rang.

"That must be the cops. I'll get it," Jackson said.

"I'm going to take some vacation time and let Cameron handle things." Jacob looped his arm around her and squeezed.

"You can't do that," Katie said. "You've worked so hard on *The Doe Hunter* case. You deserve to crack it."

"I'm worried the killer is coming after you. I won't leave you alone, and Jackson can't be with you all the time because of his family. Besides, my dad talked with Owen. He's going to meet with us."

She rested her head on Jacob's shoulder. "That's going to be an emotional rollercoaster ride."

"I'll be right there with you."

"Hey, Jacob. Katie," Officer Crane said. "Look who else decided to join the party."

"Stacey?" Katie left Jacob's embrace to give her old friend a hug. "Look at you all pregnant and whatnot."

"I know. Crazy, right?" She adjusted her gun belt. "I was headed home, and Jared called. He asked me to stop by and see if I could help."

"It's the second break-in this week," Jacob said. "The first one, they smashed her mother's picture. This time, they left one Katie's never seen before. We both have this weird feeling it could be a client of hers that is potentially my killer, but we can't figure out the connection."

"That's strange," Stacey said. "I noticed the bullet holes in the door. Did you find any casings?"

"Not a single one," Katie said.

"Have you checked the entire house? Anything else look out of place? Or damaged?"

"I searched every inch." Katie squeezed Jacob's hand a little harder. "The only thing this bastard did was leave the picture of my mom."

"Do you mind if I take a look around the house?" Stacey asked.

"Be my guest," Katie said.

"Officer Crane?" Stacey asked. "Are you okay with that?"

"I never mind working with you." Crane waved his crime scene unit in. The sheriff's office didn't have a large one, but it should do the trick for something like this. Though, Katie had to admit, she felt better that Stacey had shown up. Stacey had an eye for detail. Not that Crane didn't, but between the two of them, Katie was sure nothing would be missed.

And, of course, Jacob was by her side. Even when they'd been apart, he'd still managed to be her rock.

He stood next to her, holding her hand softly, watching the crime scene unit do their jobs. She enjoyed how his fingers laced through hers. She'd missed that connection with other human beings in general. The day Owen had finally been released from prison, she'd closed herself off from everyone—including her partner, Jackson, who'd wormed his way into her world. Jackson had become like the pesky older brother who wouldn't go away.

But she didn't miss anyone as much as she'd missed Jacob. And now she was afraid it would all be torn to bits by the past once again.

"We're going to find whoever did this, and we're going to uncover who killed your mother," Jacob whispered in her ear as if he could read where her thoughts had drifted to. He'd always been so good at reading her emotions and understanding what she needed at precisely the right moment.

"I was so hell-bent on the idea that it was my uncle that I've spent my entire adult life focused on him and not considering any other possibilities."

"So was I," Jacob said. "But I started on those files my father had. Owen basically fucked himself, leaving my dad with no defense, and my old man was—and still is—frustrated as hell that Owen did nothing to help himself."

She snapped her gaze up to meet Jacob's. "Are you serious?"

"He totally believes that going to jail saved your life, and my father knows that Owen hasn't been honest with him, but he thinks he's ready to be."

"God, I hope so. I want this nightmare to be over," she said. "Here comes Stacey."

"Did you find anything?" Jacob asked.

"I did," Stacey said. "Hey, Crane. I found a bullet casing wedged in the wooden leg of the chair in the foyer. You'll need your team to get that out and test the ballistics on it. And if you don't mind, Jared would like that report."

"I can't believe I missed that." Katie blew out a puff of air. "That's a good find. I thought I looked everywhere, and given the fact that there was a hole in the wall, I figured whoever had shot up my door was smart enough to get them all."

"Me, too. But this is lodged in pretty good," Stacey said. "For all we know, your perp was here when you got home and raced out when he heard the garage door open."

"The entire street can hear that thing," Jacob added. "So, it's possible. I'm sure you already told Crane but tell me exactly what you did when you got home."

Katie rolled her neck. "I dropped the mail on the table and immediately noticed the picture. I stared at it for a good few minutes."

"Did you touch it?" Stacey asked.

Katie shook her head. She knew better than that. "I called Jacob, and then I called the police." She also knew she should have done that in reverse, but what was done, was done. Jacob had been her first thought, and she hadn't felt as if she were in danger.

"Before you knew the front door had been blown to bits?" Stacey asked.

"Yes," Katie said. "But I knew whoever had put the picture there must have broken in somehow, so I started walking through the house. It didn't take but a few minutes to find the door. When I saw that, I just stepped outside and waited for the police."

"What door did you exit from?" Stacey asked.

"The garage," Katie said.

"Do you think you can find prints in the grass?" Jacob asked.

"Unlikely," Stacey said. "It's pretty wet out there. There are impressions, but I don't think we'll get anything good. Still, I'll have Crane's team look."

"We really appreciate it," Jacob said.

"Is it okay if Jacob and I go look through some of her family photo albums and see if we can find a picture that looks like that?" Katie asked.

Stacey nodded. "I'll let you know when Crane and his team are wrapping up."

Katie dragged Jacob through the kitchen and up the staircase into the bedroom that she used as an office and where she kept all the family albums. "This box has all the pictures from my mom's childhood. It's not a ton, so we should be able to get through them pretty quickly." She caught Jacob's gaze. "If you don't mind."

He cupped her cheek. "Of course, I don't mind." He leaned in and kissed her tenderly. "My dad offered to have us over for dinner tonight. I think we should go."

She inhaled sharply. All she'd ever wanted was answers, and now she would get the chance to ask some questions. But was she actually ready to hear what Raif had to say? "All right." She lifted the lid on the box and handed Jacob an album. "I just hope your dad doesn't give me the runaround."

"I don't think he will."

"I wish I believed that."

Jacob sat on the floor, cross-legged as he flipped through the pages. "I've been pissed at my dad for years for similar reasons. However, I believe him. He has no reason to lie to us."

Katie nodded. As much as she wanted to hold onto all that rage, she couldn't. It was time to let it go. The only purpose it'd served was to tear her and Jacob apart, and that was something she needed to fix. She'd missed him, and now that they'd reconnected, she never wanted to lose that connection again. "I just don't understand why they've let us, *me*, continue believing that my uncle might have killed my mom. Other than to tell me that there were things I didn't understand, they never really denied it." She twisted her hair and tossed it over her shoulder, joining Jacob on the floor. "Owen only sent me a few letters from prison. None of them ever denied anything. He only told me that with time, maybe I'd come to see why he had to do what he did. And that only angered me more because I thought that was some kind of confession."

"I always thought so, too." Jacob tapped a picture. "Look at this." He flipped the album.

"That was taken a few weeks before my mom was murdered."

"She's wearing the same dress, but her hair is red." Jacob pulled out his cell and tapped on the screen. He held up the image of Edward's wife that Katie had given him the other day. "My team hasn't finished the sketch of what she might look like in her youth, but the hair color is the same. As are the eyes."

"Are you suggesting that my mother is alive and is my client's missing wife?" Katie's heart lurched to the back of her throat. It stayed there and continued to pound, making it difficult to swallow.

Jacob shrugged. "My father claims that Owen didn't kill her but thought it was better if he went to jail, for your safety. Grace's body was never found."

"But there was a lot of blood. *Her* blood."

"Yeah. But there wasn't enough at the scene for the medical examiner to say that she died there."

"Doesn't matter," Jacob said as he pulled out the photo from the album. "What does bother me is that Owen never actually admitted to killing Grace. He just said he couldn't remember, and that maybe he did.

That's what killed him in court." Jacob tapped at his phone again.

"What are you doing?" she asked.

"Texting Cameron to check on the digital facial regression. I'm also asking him to give Edward's picture to everyone and see what they can find, as well as asking him to give me an update on the case."

Katie pushed the pictures aside and scooted closer. She leaned, cupping his face and gently pressed her lips against his mouth, letting them linger for a long moment. "I don't want you to give up that case. It could be the biggest of your career."

"Four years ago, I made the biggest mistake of my life, and I'm not going to let history repeat itself," he said. "You are more important to me than any case. I'd rather lose my job than lose you again."

She closed her eyes and took in a deep breath before blinking them open. "We do have to talk about Hannah and what she did."

"You have to know I didn't tell her anything."

"I want to believe you, Jacob." She dropped her hands to her lap. "But how did she find out about the baby we lost and the circumstances of my miscarriage. She all but made it sound like it was my fault, and that you blamed me."

"I never blamed you. If anything, I blamed myself for not being there for you that day, and I told her that. Hell, that's basically how I ended up with that crazy woman."

"You got to me as soon as you could."

"It wasn't soon enough," Jacob said. "You hadn't been feeling well that morning and were spotting. I shouldn't have left you alone to begin with. Just because I was going to be in court that day with opening arguments was no excuse. Someone else could have done them."

She palmed his cheek. "We had no idea I was going to miscarry, but it was private, something between us. We hadn't even told anyone I was pregnant."

"My parents were pretty shocked watching that on the news," he admitted. "My mother didn't speak to me for a week."

"She sent me the prettiest flower arrangement, but it's not just that. Hannah knew things about me that only you would have known, and then she put her own spin on them, making me look like a crazy bitch. How did she find all that stuff out?"

Jacob ran a hand over his face and let out a long breath. "The short time I was with her, I never wanted her in my apartment. I couldn't stand the idea of anyone else being there but you. Only, one time I let her stay, and I found her going through my things. That's when I ended it. A week later, she did the story on you. I'd never been so angry in my life. I marched myself down to the station and got myself thrown out. Had I not been an assistant to the District Attorney, I might have gotten arrested."

"Well, thank you for that," Katie said.

"I no longer think we need you to do that interview with Hannah. We're connecting the dots just fine by ourselves."

"I don't know. Maybe it's time I do it. And if I do it live, she can't control my narrative. Not only that, but I also don't have to make it exclusive," Katie said.

"You might not want to hear this, but I think we should run it by my dad."

"That's not a bad idea, especially since I don't want to do it until after I've talked to him and Owen." She stood, taking the albums and stacking them neatly in the box. It felt like such a treat to take them out.

Jacob hopped to his feet. "I've been meaning to talk to you about the victim profiler. He had some interesting things to say about my killer and the kind of girls he goes after."

"Yeah. What's that?"

"For starters, he doesn't believe the man is killing the same person over and over again."

"But all his victims are redheads."

"The profiler believes this guy is simply a hunter. Like the name he's been given. He just has a type of woman he likes to hunt, and he's proud of his kills. It's as if he's displaying them as his trophies so the world can see what he's done."

"That's sick." She hugged herself and shivered.

Jacob wrapped her in his strong arms. "Another reason I'm not leaving your side until he's caught. I'm afraid he might be the one who is fucking with you."

8

Jacob made the executive decision to have him and Katie spend the night at his parents' house until he could replace the front door.

Again.

Katie hadn't liked the idea, but Jackson helped talk her into it, and it would only be for a couple of days.

"Your parents' place always looks so amazing, but damn those fake fireworks are bright."

Jacob laughed as the garage door opened and his mother's ugly green Crocs shuffled across the cement floor.

"Does she ever wear anything else around the house?" Katie asked.

"Not that I can remember." Jacob grabbed the door handle. "Just remember that the anniversary of Jonathon's death is next week."

"I'll be careful with what I say."

"Thanks," Jacob said. "She seems pretty happy this year, but you know how she can get."

Katie reached across the Jeep and squeezed his arm. "She loves you. She's just afraid."

"I know." Jacob had heard it his entire life, how his mother had been so terrified that Jacob might die too somehow, and that instead of smothering him or being overprotective, she responded by keeping him at a safe distance. He'd seen a few therapists over the years, and they'd all said the same thing. It wasn't common, but it did happen, and all he could do was show his mom kindness and love.

And that's what he'd done.

However, he still felt a sense of loneliness, and he missed his mother.

He pulled open the door and was greeted with a big bear hug. His mom almost didn't let go.

That was unusual.

"Hey, Mom." He held her for a long moment. "Is something wrong?"

"Your father told me what happened." She looked up at him with tears in her eyes. "I'm just so glad you and Katie are okay." She rose on tiptoe and kissed his cheek before racing around the hood and doing the same to Katie.

She looked at him with wide eyes as she embraced his mother. "Hi, Mrs. Donovan."

"Please, call me Isabelle," his mother said. "Now,

let's get the two of you inside. I opened a nice bottle of red wine, and I made an apple pie. Your father's going to get a fire started in the backyard so we can enjoy this beautiful night. So glad the temperatures are finally warming up again." She looped her arm through Katie's and dragged her into the garage.

Jacob snagged his duffle and Katie's and then followed two paces behind, wondering if his mother had gotten an early start on the wine.

"I made up both guest rooms, but if you two are back together, you don't have to use both. Your father and I are okay if you want to share a room. We're not that old-fashioned."

Jacob chuckled. "You never quit, do you?"

"And you're avoiding my question." His mother turned and grinned.

"You didn't ask one." He cocked his head as he set the bags on the bench. "Besides, I'm not sure Katie appreciates—"

"*Katie* can speak for herself." Katie squeezed his arm. "It's actually up to Jacob if we share a room or not. The ball's kind of in his court right now."

"It most certainly is not." Jacob glared. He couldn't believe he was having this conversation in front of his mother, for starters. But, seriously, he'd told Katie that he still loved her, and she'd yet to say the words back. "You know where I stand. You're the one—"

"We'll share a room," Katie said softly. "Thank you for your hospitality, Isabelle. I really appreciate it."

"Wait until Raif hears that the two of you are back together. He's going to flip." His mother turned on her heels without putting on her slippers and raced off to find his dad.

"So, are we a couple?" Jacob asked. "Because that's what I'd like."

"Let's just say this is a test drive." Katie patted his chest and laughed. "I have to admit. Your mother is about the only person on this planet that can embarrass me."

"Your cheeks did turn a little red." Jacob looped his arm around her shoulders and guided her through the house and out onto the back patio, where he found his mother having an animated conversation with his old man. It warmed his heart to see his parents happy. He knew they had a good relationship. They had to, in order to survive the loss of a child and, of course, the scandal created by Katie's uncle and mother.

As mad as Jacob had gotten at his dad, he'd always respected him as both a dad and a lawyer—but especially as a husband. He'd stood by his mother during her darkest hour. Jacob had just been a little boy, but he remembered the days when all his mother did was cry herself to sleep at night. She'd try to put on a brave face as she held his hand and walked him to the bus stop. Or when she came to school on her volunteer days. She'd always been there for him; she just hadn't been as present as some of the other mothers.

His father glanced in their direction as Jacob

stepped out into the backyard that overlooked the dark waters of Lake George. His parents lived on Cleverdale, not far from the marina, about five houses north of Jared Blake's house. As a kid, he used to sit out on his dock and stare at the Bateman estate, wondering if Katie would ever return. He'd been a few years older, but he remembered playing at her house, and her at his.

"I'm so glad you two took us up on our offer." His father gave him a manly hug and kissed Katie on the cheek. "I'm so sorry that all of this is happening to you."

"Why don't you both take a seat and have some wine?" his mother said. "I'll go get that apple pie. I've also got some other snacks prepared in case you wanted something or hadn't eaten dinner yet."

"Of course, you do, Mom." Jacob took the glass his mother offered and made himself comfortable in the loveseat next to Katie. Flames crackled in the glass stones of the fire pit.

His father sat in one of the big lounge chairs. He put his feet up and took out a cigar. "Would you like one, son?"

"God, no. The last time I smoked one of those, I was in college, and it made me sicker than a dog." Jacob swirled his wine and stared at the red liquid as it hugged the sides.

"I don't mean to dive right into a touchy subject," Katie said, "but have you spoken to my uncle today?"

His father leaned forward. "As a matter of fact, I spoke with him about fifteen minutes before you showed up. If you're up for it, he'd like to come over in the morning."

"That would be okay with me." Katie placed her hand on Jacob's leg and squeezed.

Jacob covered it with his. He could feel uncertainty seeping from her skin to his. He understood her apprehension. "What have you told him about what's going on?"

"Everything," his father admitted. "And you should know that Hannah woman is hounding him like a lion on the hunt. She's relentless. She's cornered him a few times, and she's always trying to bait him into saying something stupid."

"I'm not surprised," Jacob said. "We're no longer sure if we should do the interview. There have been some developments in the case."

"What can you tell me?" his father asked.

"Maybe we should wait until my uncle is here." Katie glanced at Jacob, catching his gaze as if to look for confirmation. "I've been working on a missing person's case that might have collided with Jacob's murder investigation and my mother's disappearance in a peculiar way."

"I've heard a little bit about that, but Jacob hasn't given me a lot of details," his father said. "I'm sure you want to know more about what's in my files since you haven't had a chance to make it to my office."

Just then, his mother returned with a decadent apple pie and a plate full of other goodies like little sandwiches, wraps, chips, dip, and veggies. She had enough food to feed a small army.

As usual.

His therapist had once told him that his mom showed her unconditional love for him in other ways.

And this was one.

He leaned forward and filled a plate with a couple of turkey sandwiches, cucumbers, and dip. He'd dig into that pie after he polished off a few other things.

Like that chicken wing dip, which Katie went straight for.

His mother settled into the chair next to her husband and tucked her feet under her butt as she sipped her wine.

"Feel free to ask me whatever you want," his father said.

Katie glanced between Jacob and her father.

"It's okay. She knows everything," his father said. "And when I say everything, I mean that. We have no secrets. She was with me through the entire trial. Through all the accusations. And when our beloved Jonathon died during all of it, she was still right there by my side. It took a toll on all of us, but we did what we thought was best at the time."

Jacob inhaled sharply and coughed. It was rare that they ever openly spoke about his brother. Or at least, *he* never did for fear of making his mother cry. She'd done that a lot, at least from what he could remember from when he was a young boy. As he got older, he'd learned not to speak of his brother unless his parents broached the subject. While that happened regularly at holidays, birthdays, and the anniversary of his death, he never allowed himself to dig too deeply into things with his mom. He couldn't bear the thought of making her cry.

"I know it upsets you to talk about him." His mother wiped a stray tear. "He would have been thirty-eight this year." She shook her head.

Katie squeezed Jacob's hand, and he held on for dear life. He had no idea what to say or how to respond. When he and his mother discussed Jonathon, she'd always been so distant with Jacob.

This felt different.

"I wish I remembered more about him." Jacob let a small smile form on his lips. "I always wanted to be just like him. Next to Dad, he was my hero."

"You used to follow him around, dragging your little Batman cape. Jonathon would act all frustrated, but deep down, he loved that you idolized him," his father said. "What do you remember from the fire?"

Jacob shook his head. It wasn't that he couldn't believe they were having this conversation. It was more that his mother was fully present and not crying her eyes out. Especially given that it was so close to the anniversary. It had his jaw gaping. "I just remember someone lifting me from my bed and carrying me outside. There were sirens and people shouting, and I remember the house burning. There were flames everywhere, and it was hot. Really hot. And I was drenched as if I'd been in a bathtub. But I always wondered if those were real memories or just things I saw in news coverage years later. I was only seven years old."

"Those are all real memories," his father said. "But do you remember who helped you out of the house?"

Jacob shook his head. "I assume a fireman." He'd read the articles about the fire, but everyone had been focused on the trial and Owen more than they were on the tragedy that had struck Jacob's family. Perhaps that had been a good thing.

Or maybe a curse that kept his family in this perpetual state of limbo.

His mother sat up a little taller and swiped at her face. "Your therapist always told us that we needed to let the memories come to you naturally, so we never pushed. But the further you drifted from me, the more I wanted to tell you. My psychologist at the time didn't think it was a good idea. She thought it might be too much for you to handle."

"Mom. What are you talking about?"

She scooted to the edge of her seat. "The therapists worried about survivor's guilt with you. As did your father and me. But you're not a child anymore, and I'm tired of us dancing around each other like there is some wedge between us." She cleared her throat. "You and Jonathon were having one of your *sleepovers* that night, but at about one in the morning, you had a nightmare."

"We assumed Jonathon let you watch a scary movie by the way you came screaming into our bedroom," his father said.

"I remember that, and you put me back in my room." Jacob's heart tightened.

"We did," his mother admitted. "A few hours later, we heard the fire alarm going off. The house was already filled with thick, black smoke. We couldn't open the bedroom door, it was so hot in the hallway. Your dad had to break a window, and that's when we saw you standing in the front yard with your Batman cape."

"Alone?" Katie asked.

"A fire truck had just rolled up, and one of the firefighters was with him," his mother said. "Once we were rescued, we found out that it was Jonathon who'd helped Jacob out of the house then went back in to get us. The fireman said he literally jumped from the moving vehicle to try and stop him, but it was too late, and—"

"Jonathon never made it back out." Tears formed in Jacob's eyes. All these years, he'd thought it was his mom who had pulled away from him, when in reality, his mother had been giving him space to cope with the death of his brother and being the one who'd survived.

After his brother had saved him.

Jacob leaned forward and swiped at his cheeks. "Why didn't you ever tell me this?"

"At first, you were so young that we thought it

would further traumatize you." His mother stood and gracefully made her way across the patio. She pulled up another chair and put her arm around Jacob. "As you got older, we didn't know what you remembered and you never wanted to talk about it."

He stared into his mother's eyes. "I didn't want to make you cry."

She cupped his cheeks. Tears flowed freely down her face, taking a glob of mascara with them. "You never made me weep. You always brought me joy, and I'm sorry that I made you feel that way. Especially in the early years."

"Son, please understand the only reason we never told you that Jonathon was the one who brought you out of the house was because we didn't want to cause you any more pain than you were already going through," his father said. "And then, after years of not doing so, we felt it was best to leave it alone."

Jacob nodded as he pulled his mother in for a hug. All the distance he'd once felt vanished in an instant.

Of course, it had never really been there, except for in his mind. "I'm sorry, Mom. I never meant to push you away."

"You did no such thing." His mother kissed his cheek. "Now, while I'm grateful we cleared all that up, I know you have more pressing business to discuss." She took the bottle of wine and topped off everyone's glasses. "Another topic we shouldn't have kept from either of you."

Jacob wrapped his arm around Katie and pulled her close.

She leaned in, hugged his middle, and rested her head on his shoulder. "We can do this tomorrow," she said.

"You've waited a long time for answers," his father said. "If I can help give you some, I want to do that. And maybe prepare you for meeting with your uncle tomorrow."

"Why do I need to be prepared?" Katie sat up straight and took a gulp of wine before cutting into the pie.

She wasn't really hungry, but if she didn't eat, she'd drink.

And getting drunk wasn't an option.

Raif lifted his cigar and took a puff. He blew a big smoke ring. "I tried to save Owen from himself, but he wouldn't help in his defense. The only thing he wouldn't do was confess."

"Thank God for that," Isabelle said. "He might never have gotten out if he did."

"Well, yesterday, he wished he was still in jail." Raif put out his cigar and shifted in his seat. "He believes everything that is happening now is his fault."

"A week ago, I thought the same thing," Katie

muttered. "What other evidence wasn't allowed into court?" She was too tired to beat around the bush.

"There was a witness," Raif said.

"To what, exactly?" Jacob asked.

Katie tried to swallow, but her muscles wouldn't work. Her heart pounded so hard and fast, she wasn't sure she'd be able to breathe. She took her fist to her chest and gave it a little pound. "And who?" she whispered.

"A couple of teenagers were fishing off the point," Raif said. "They said they saw a man that wasn't Owen shove Grace into a car and drive off. The timeframe adds up, and I had a chance to speak to the kids. They were adamant that there was another man."

"Didn't the cops interview them?" Jacob asked.

Raif shook his head. "My investigator found them, but when it came time for the trial, I couldn't put them on the stand. The district attorney found other witnesses who saw them drinking and getting high, and their parents didn't want them to get involved. I've since talked to them, and they stand by their story."

"Do you think they'd be willing to take a look at a photograph of my client?" Katie couldn't believe how much had been suppressed in her uncle's trial. But what still confused her is why on earth did Owen believe that she was safer with him in jail? That would be her first question tomorrow.

"I'm sure they would. I'll contact them first thing in the morning." Raif nibbled on some cheese and a cracker. He always carried himself in a relaxed manner, no matter the atmosphere—including court. Katie had seen him in action a few times. She actually questioned how he'd lost her uncle's case.

But now it made perfect sense.

"Any other evidence we don't know about?" Jacob asked.

"There are a few little things. But you also have to look at the lack of evidence in this case," Raif said. "However, the real frustrating thing right now is what has been happening to you. Even though I know I can prove that Owen had nothing to do with it, the press, and especially Hannah, are having a field day with it."

Katie glanced at Jacob. "We didn't see the news tonight, did something happen?"

"Oh, boy," Raif said. "For starters, she mentioned that the FBI was working with the locals on a string of new murders. She did her homework and attached a couple of older cases to yours and then she all but called you incompetent."

Jacob laughed. "I'm shocked her producers and station give her such a long leash."

"I wonder how accurate her information on both the past and present murders is?" Katie asked. "And where is she getting her intel?"

"I haven't deleted the news yet if you want to watch it," Raif said.

"Why the hell would I want to do that?" Jacob

leaned back and looped his arm over the back of the bench. "I don't give a shit what that woman says."

"Katie has a point," Isabelle said. "If she has facts about the case that you don't want the public to know—"

"Cameron would have texted or called." Jacob patted the front of his pants. And then the back. "Shit. I must have left my cell in my vehicle." He stood. "I'll be right back."

"Why don't we take this inside?" Raif hit a remote button, and the fire quickly died down. "Even if his partner didn't try to reach him, I know my son's going to want to see this."

"I might not rewatch." Isabelle let out a short breath as she gathered a few plates. "I might toss something at the television again."

"You might have to restrain me," Katie said.

"I wouldn't dream of it." Isabelle offered a smile. "I can't stand Hannah. So, feel free to let out whatever you have to. That woman is a snake. She once tried to turn our tragedy into a story."

Katie snagged a tray and opened the sliding glass door. "What do you mean?"

"She had the nerve to come to me and ask for an interview about the fire. I nearly strangled her right there," Isabelle said. "She tried to play it up like she wanted to do some kind of human-interest piece, but I knew her real motive was to dig into our dark secrets."

"She's a real piece of work." Katie set the tray on the

middle of the kitchen island. "But I'm like a deer in headlights. I don't know why I keep watching her news specials."

"Raif has to watch them all the time." Isabelle took Katie by the hand and led her into the family room, where Jacob met them with a crinkled forehead.

"Cameron did try to reach me, and Hannah has some intel that we didn't leak to the press."

"Do you want me to hit play?" his father asked, holding the remote.

Jacob shook his head. "I don't really need to watch it. But if Katie wants to, that's fine."

"Does she talk about me?" Katie asked.

"No. But she does say that Jacob is about as bad of an FBI agent as I was a lawyer for not being able to defend your uncle properly, and she called my wife—"

"I'd rather not go there," Isabelle said.

"Mom. Did you think my partner would spare my feelings?" Jacob took an apple from the fruit bowl. "And for the record, I never described you as a heartless mother."

"She said that?" Katie had seen Hannah go low, but never *that* low. "What the hell is Hannah thinking? That's not reporting a human-interest story. That's slander."

"Well, Cameron is picking her up and bringing her downtown. I want to be there for that." Jacob gave Katie a quick kiss on the forehead. "Don't wait up for me. I could be pretty late. What time is Owen coming over?"

"He said he'd be here around nine," Raif said.

"I'll make sure I'm back." Jacob turned on his heels and headed back out the door.

So much for him taking time off work. But Katie actually understood why he wanted to be at the interview.

Once again, too many seemingly separate cases were colliding.

"Can I ask you a question?" Katie caught Raif's gaze.

"Of course."

"Do you think my mother could still be alive?"

"Anything is possible," Raif said. "And it's something that your uncle and I have talked about. But she loved you, and she wouldn't have left you, not willingly, at least, for any length of time."

"One more thing," Katie said. "Do you have any idea who my father is?"

"Not a clue." Raif reached out and squeezed her shoulder. "When Grace first returned home, you were about a year old. She wouldn't talk about your father or what'd happened, but both Owen and I thought that something wasn't right. About six months before she disappeared, she became erratic in her behavior. She was secretive, and she left twice for a couple of weeks, leaving you in your uncle's care."

"Where did she go?" Katie asked.

"We don't know. But she was dating someone."

"Who?"

"Another thing we don't know," Raif said. "When she came back the second time, she acted as if Owen were the enemy." Raif shook his head. "There is no way Owen hurt his sister. All he wanted to do was help her out of whatever trouble she'd gotten herself into, and with her suffering from bipolar depression, that became tricky. When she took money out of her account, we knew something was going on, and we both tried to talk to her. I was seen out and about with her a few times, and that's probably how the rumors started about us having an affair. But they were squashed pretty quickly when my son died."

"Until Hannah brought them back up," Katie said. "At first, I thought she did half of this bullcrap just to hurt me or Jacob, but now it feels like someone is feeding her the stories."

"Raif was saying exactly the same thing." Isabelle leaned into her husband. "Owen returning to Lake George has some people on edge."

"But it's more than that. And I think it has to do with Jacob's murder case."

9

Jacob entered the federal building in downtown Albany at about ten in the evening. He pushed the elevator button aggressively as if that would make it show up faster.

Cameron had promised that he'd wait for him before he began questioning Hannah, which would only make her more agitated. And when she felt backed into a corner, she came out swinging. Might not be a bad approach. Because when she was that angry, she said and did things that tended to get her into trouble.

Once inside the elevator, Jacob stared at the ceiling and inhaled sharply. He needed to remain calm.

He'd promised Katie in a text that he wouldn't lose his cool and say or do something that could give Hannah something to put on the evening news. Of course, she was about to get slapped with an injunction and perhaps a night in jail if she didn't reveal her source—or at least he hoped the court order had come through.

Stepping into the hallway, he nearly bumped right into Cameron.

"Hey, man. You made good time." Cameron slapped him on the back. "We put Hannah in room two. She's not happy."

"Good," Jacob said.

"And we got the warrant." Cameron waved a piece of paper. "Though if I can be so bold to suggest it, I say we don't show our hand right away."

"I'm down with that." Jacob tried to control his raging heartbeat, but it proved to be impossible. "How do you want to play this?"

"Up to you. You know her better than I do, so I'm cool if you want to question her."

Jacob rubbed his temples. He really wanted to take a crack at her, but he worried he wouldn't be able to hold his tongue, especially after finding out that she'd come after his mother. His family and their business was off-limits, especially the death of his brother. "I need you to call me off if I start hitting below the belt."

"I can do that." Cameron pushed open the door to the interrogation room.

Hannah sat at the table with her hands in her lap. She glanced at the door, and her mouth gaped open. "Really? I have to be questioned by him?" She stuck her thumb out and made a jerking motion. "I'd rather be waterboarded."

Jacob ignored her complaints and took the folder that Cameron handed him as he sat across from Hannah. All that was inside were some hand-scribbled notes along with the transcript of her newscast. "I'm going to make this quick and painless," he said. "Who told you about the position of the bodies or that they were moved?"

"I'm not giving away my source." Hannah folded her arms.

"And what if your source got it wrong?"

For a brief second, Hannah's eyes went wide. "I don't believe you."

She was right. Her source was spot-on in what he'd told her, and Jacob wasn't going to spend too much time denying it. The damage had been done. There was no taking it back in the press.

"Why didn't you try to verify with my office? And don't tell me you did because we both know you didn't," Jacob said.

"I didn't need to." She tilted her head and smiled. "My source is one of you."

"No one in my office would give you even a second glance." Jacob hated playing games, and Hannah was a master. She'd do anything to deflect and avoid answering his questions. But there was no way she was even being remotely truthful right now.

"I never said my source was from this building. I just said it's one of you." She winked.

"Oh, for fuck's sake, Hannah. Let's stop this bullshit.

Who told you about the staging of the victims? For the record, we're not afraid to toss you in jail for obstruction of justice."

"You can't make me give up a source."

"This warrant can." He slapped the paper on the table.

She leaned over and glanced between the warrant, Cameron, and Jacob. She blinked as she tucked her hair behind her ears. "I thought you wanted the information leaked."

"Now why the hell would we want that?" Cameron asked. "Besides creating a panic, we run the risk of copycats. Not to mention, it just makes it harder for us to catch our bad guy when we're stuck in this room with the likes of you."

"Your visiting agent told me he wanted to use me to flush out the killer," Hannah said. A frown replaced her cocky smile.

"What's the agent's name?" Jacob asked.

"Thurston Howell."

Jacob exchanged looks with Cameron. "We don't have anyone by that name," Jacob said as he pulled out his cell.

Katie's client's name was Edward Howell.

That couldn't be a coincidence.

"He had a badge. And I've seen him hanging out in different places. I even saw him talking with Katie and Jackson after he mentioned following her uncle for a different reason."

"Is this him?" Jacob pushed his phone in front of her.

"Yes. That's him. I thought—"

"Stop thinking, Hannah," Jacob said. "It's not a good look." He stood. "I want a detail over at my old man's house ASAP, and I want them on Katie at all times."

Cameron nodded.

"And you." He pointed at Hannah. "If this man contacts you again, I want you to call Cameron right away."

"I'd feel more comfortable if I could call you." She batted her lashes. "This has me scared now."

Jacob wanted to laugh, only he couldn't even stomach a sarcastic one. As a federal officer, he'd do his duty and protect all citizens. And that meant Hannah. But he wasn't going to be at her beck and call. "Too bad," Jacob said. "You lost that right the second you came at my mom. Stay away from me, Katie, and my family. And do the right fucking thing for a change." He glanced at Cameron. "Take her official statement. Find out when and where she met with him and when the last time was that she saw him. Don't let her leave until your detailed brain is satisfied that you have everything."

"That might take all night," Cameron said with a big smile.

"I'm good with that." Until one of his agents could get to his parents' house, he was going to call in a favor.

"Jacob. You don't mean that." Hannah glared. "Consider everything we've been through."

"You mean what you put me through." He raked a hand across his head. "If you hear from this Thurston guy, I want you to call Cameron immediately. Don't do anything stupid, okay?"

She nodded.

Jacob took off toward the elevators and sent a text to Jared Blake in hopes that he'd have a State Trooper he could put on Rockhurst Road.

His next call would be to Jackson.

And then Katie.

She wouldn't take this news sitting down, so he'd better warn his old man so he could make sure Katie stayed put.

Jacob locked the garage door and kicked off his shoes before padding through the family room and stopping in the kitchen for a water bottle, where he found his father sitting at the table cupping a mug of tea. "There was no need to wait up."

"I couldn't sleep thinking about this Edward or Thurston fellow," his father said. "Do you really think he could be *The Doe Killer*?"

"If not, he's one hell of a copycat." Jacob leaned against the counter and swigged his aqua. Water had never tasted so good. "Are you sure you've never seen him?"

His father nodded. "Your mother thinks she might have seen him at the grocery store, but she can't be sure."

"That scares me," Jacob said. "This guy could be watching all of us. Did you say anything to Owen about him?"

"You didn't tell me to, so I thought it best to wait until you did." His father lifted his gaze. "I know Owen didn't do anything wrong all those years ago. And I know everything he's doing now, he believes he's doing to protect Katie and the rest of us. However, he's misguided, and I'm afraid he'll go off and do something crazy if I give him too much."

"Thanks. I appreciate that. It's probably best if I handle this part." Jacob pinched the bridge of his nose. "But you get that all these secrets have only made my job harder, right?"

"I do get that, but we did what we thought was best. And up until Owen was released, I'd do it all exactly the same way," his father said. "This psychopath has been killing young women for three decades." His father dunked the tea bag and then twisted it around the spoon. He squeezed a lemon wedge into his drink and stirred. "Do you think it started with Grace?"

"I don't think so. There are some unsolved cases that appear as if they could be early kills." Jacob shook his head. "I believe Grace is the one he couldn't kill."

"And why is that?"

Jacob stared at his father with an arched brow.

"You really think he could be Katie's father?"

"That's the only thing that makes any sense to me." Bile rose from deep in Jacob's gut at hearing his father say the words that he'd barely allowed himself to think.

"That means Grace is alive," his father said so faintly, Jacob had to strain to hear. Still, the gravity of his statement squeezed his heart.

"At least, I believe she was when Owen was arrested, but I can't be so sure now."

His father snapped his head, catching Jacob's gaze. "Then why would he come looking for her?"

"To fuck with Katie. For all we know, he murdered her shortly after they married. I mean, I keep asking myself... Why did he come back now? What makes this timeframe so special? Owen was released two years ago. He's been living here for a few months. It's not the anniversary of anything. So why?"

"Maybe she really is missing. Maybe she's been a hostage all these years and finally managed to escape," his father said.

"He did tell Katie that she'd taken something he wanted." Jacob rubbed the back of his neck. "It's seriously fucking twisted to use his own daughter like that."

"Grace never talked about Katie's father. When she first came back, she said that he was dead to her and that he didn't want to be a father to Katie. So, we let it go. We figured she was better off without him."

"Owen's never wagered a guess?"

Jacob's father let out a long breath. "He often wondered if maybe it was someone close to home, and the father was a married man or something. I mean, Grace didn't have the best taste in men, and she wanted so desperately to be taken care of." His father pounded his fist on the table. "For the last day or two, Owen has been unusually vague, which pisses me right the fuck off. Either something happened, or Owen knows something, and he's not sharing."

"Why do you say that?" Jacob asked.

"He's been acting nervous and avoiding coming to see me."

"Well, he'd better damn well come clean tomorrow, or he's going to have to answer to me." Jacob polished off his water. "I need to go check on Katie. Knowing her, she paced a hole in Mom's carpet, waiting for me to come up."

His father stood and placed a firm hand on his shoulder. "Katie is a good woman, and she loves you. Don't fuck it up again."

Jacob let out a short chuckle. "I love her, too. And I don't plan on it."

"Good." His father reached into his pocket. "I know this is premature, but your mother asked me to give this to you." He held out a small black velvet box. "It's your grandmother's engagement ring."

Jacob swallowed his pounding heart. He opened his mouth but only a grunt formed. He cleared his throat. "I'd say that's a little presumptuous." Of course, there was only one person he pictured himself marrying, and that was Katie. She was his soul mate. She was the only person in his life that truly understood him, and he wanted to spend the rest of his life showing her how important she was to him. "I'm not even sure if she sees us as being back together or not."

"If she's willing to share a bedroom at your parents' house, I'd say that's a move in that direction."

"Katie is also known for being efficient. It's one way to keep me close so she can make sure I tell her everything in a timely manner, and Mom doesn't have to wash two sets of sheets when we leave." Jacob lifted the top of the box and peeked in. His mother had always told him that the ring would be there when he was ready to propose.

Only, she'd taken that back when he'd dated Hannah. His mother had mentioned that the only woman worthy of her mother's ring was Katie.

Jacob had to agree.

The marquis-shaped diamond sparkled in the dim lighting. Staring at it gave Jacob butterflies in his gut. He loved Katie more than anything and would do whatever it took to keep her in his life.

Anything.

He closed the box. "When this happens, I hope Katie doesn't want some big fancy wedding."

His father smiled. "Look at you, saying 'when' instead of 'if.'"

Jacob shook his head. "I never stopped loving her, we both just got lost." He locked gazes with his old man. "In part because of these legacies of lies that both of our families left behind. We can't have that anymore, okay?"

"Everything I know, or your mother knows, we've told you. I promise."

Jacob nodded. For the first time in a long while, he actually believed his dad. "I'll see you in the morning." He stuffed the ring into his pocket and made his way up the stairs to his old bedroom.

His parents had bought this house two months after his brother had died. They hadn't wanted to rebuild the old one and be constantly reminded of their loss. The family that ended up buying the lot built a home so different, that Jacob had all but forgotten. However, maybe that hadn't been such a good thing since he hadn't remembered his brother helping him out of the house.

Had he known, he and his mother might have had a better relationship.

As he rounded the corner, a few memories from his childhood bombarded his brain. He smiled. Jonathon always tried to act like the cooler older brother, especially around his friends. But whenever they were alone, Jonathon was Jacob's best friend.

Tears welled in Jacob's eyes. He pressed his hand against the wall and stood in the middle of the hallway.

He remembered his brother shaking him awake, and the roar of the fire filled his memory as if he were there.

"Jacob. Wake up. We have to get out of the house," Jonathon said.

"What?" Jacob wiped his eyes and rolled over.

"Let's go." Jonathon yanked his arm so hard, Jacob fell to the floor. "We have to get Mom and Dad. Stay close behind me."

Jacob grabbed his Batman cape and held his brother's hand. Tight. They made it to the hallway but couldn't go any farther. Water poured from the ceiling, but it did nothing to prevent the flames from climbing up the wall and engulfing the path toward his parents' room.

"We have to get outside." Jonathon tugged him down the stairs. Flames jumped out at them as if they were trying to catch them. Twice, Jacob's clothes caught fire and Jonathon tossed him to the floor and rolled on him.

Jonathon pushed him out the door and into the front yard. "Can you hear the fire trucks?"

Jacob nodded as he stared at the house. It was so bright and hot it burned his eyes.

"Stay here. I'm going in through the garage and the service staircase. I can get to Mom and Dad that way."

"Don't go, Jonathon." Jacob cried. "I'm scared."

"Me, too. But I don't see them, and I have to help them."

A second later, Jonathon was running toward the garage as a fireman screamed at him to stop.

Less than a minute later, the garage roof caved in, and Jacob heard his parents yelling from their bedroom window.

But not Jonathon.

Jacob rubbed his eyes, and the memory etched into his mind. He'd never forget again.

Jonathon had saved him. Had it not been for his brother, Jacob would have surely perished in that fire.

They all would have.

Jacob blew out a puff of air. He understood why his mother had given him space. That would have been a lot for a seven-year-old to handle.

However, he'd have to find ways to show his mom just how much she mattered in his childhood.

And even more so now.

"Hey, you," Katie said as she leaned against the doorjamb wearing his T-shirt tied in a knot at her waist and his FBI workout shorts.

She'd never looked sexier.

"Boy are you a sight for sore eyes." He closed the gap and brushed her soft, red hair from her face before kissing her lips tenderly.

He heard his father's footsteps coming up the stairs.

But he didn't care.

She wrapped her arms around his shoulders, deepening the kiss. Their tongues danced in an old, familiar yet passionate waltz. They fit together like the moon and the stars in the night sky.

"Good night, children," his father said with a bit of laughter in his tone.

Katie dropped her head to his chest. "Sleep well, Raif," she whispered.

Jacob took her by the hand and led them into his room. His parents hadn't changed his room since he'd moved out for good. It still had the same queen-sized bed with dark plaid covers. All his trophies from high school and college were still displayed proudly on the shelves that his father had built. "What have you been doing since I called on the way home?"

"Staring at that picture of Edward, looking for similarities between him and me."

"Find any?" He lifted his shirt over his head and tossed it onto the back of the chair in front of his old computer desk.

"Not really. I'm the spitting image of my mother for the most part."

"Most people will tell you that Jonathon looked more like my dad than I do."

"From the pictures you showed me, I'd have to agree." She splayed her hand over his bare back. "You've always favored your mom."

"Just what a man wants to hear." He kissed her temple before slipping out of his pants and folding them over the chair, as well.

The jewelry box fell to the floor.

"Shit," he mumbled as he bent over, but Katie beat him to the punch.

"What's this?" She held the small velvet box in her hand.

He scratched the back of his head. "It's my grandmother's ring."

"What kind of ring?"

"Do I really need to say that out loud, or do you think you can figure it out?"

Katie glanced between the little black box in her hands and Jacob. "What are you doing with it?"

This conversation would be interesting. He'd promised himself that he'd never lie to Katie again. And he'd meant it.

So, he couldn't do it now. Even when it came to an engagement ring.

"My mom gave it to my dad to give to me," Jacob admitted.

Katie cocked her head. "Why would she do that?"

"So that I'd have it for whenever I was ready to give it to you."

She blinked. About a dozen or so times in rapid succession. "You asked her for this?"

"No. I did not." He planted his hands on his hips and stared at Katie dead-on. He swallowed his pounding heart. He loved this woman more than he loved anything else. He would move heaven and earth to give her whatever she needed or wanted. Hell, if she asked, he'd quit his job and find something closer to home. Of course, he considered doing that anyway for a variety of reasons, her being the biggest one. "But I would have soon enough."

She fingered the top. "Can I look at it?"

He shrugged. "Be my guest."

Slowly, she opened the lid and gasped. "Oh, my God. It's gorgeous. I've never seen anything so big or beautiful before."

"Why don't you try it on?" He reached out and took the box from her trembling hand. Lifting the ring, he eased it onto her ring finger.

"I can't believe you're doing that right now."

"Me, neither, but look. It's a perfect fit." He thumbed the diamond. "I do love you, Katie. I never stopped, and I will love you forever. I want to get married someday. Definitely sooner rather than later, but I know it's been a long time since we've been a couple, and you need time to—"

"I love you, too, Jacob." She palmed his cheek. "I know I've been hard on you."

"I deserved it." He toyed with the drawstring on her shorts. "So, you still love me?"

She smiled. "Did you have any doubts?"

"Maybe a few."

"Perhaps this will make sure you never forget." Quickly, she removed her top and shorts and stood in front of him in only a tiny pair of boy shorts. She pressed her lips against his skin and kissed her way down his stomach, making his muscles twitch.

Sticking her fingers into the elastic of his underwear, she rolled them over his hips.

"What are you doing?" he asked with a throaty voice as he piled her thick hair on the top of her head.

"What does it look like?"

He stepped out of his undergarments and groaned as she took him in her hands, stroking gently with her soft palms.

When most people looked at Katie, they saw a tough-as-nails girl with a hard-ass attitude who'd been through hell and back. But Jacob saw so much more.

Katie was a kind and loving woman who, when she gave herself, did so completely.

His breathing became erratic when she licked her lips and then licked him, slowly taking his length into her mouth. He couldn't fill his lungs if he tried. A twinge of jealousy for any man who might have been with her during their breakup filled his heart.

He only had himself to blame for that, and he'd forever try to make up for that mistake. "Come here," he whispered.

She stood, wrapping her arms around his shoulders and pressing her mouth over his in a wild, passionate kiss.

He'd lost his ability to think straight. All he wanted was to fill and satisfy her until he left her breathless.

Swiftly, he removed her panties and lifted her, pressing her against the wall.

She clasped her feet around his back as he thrust

inside her, desperate to feel their bodies tangled as though they were one body. One mind.

Her nails dug into his shoulders as she slammed her head against the wall. "Yes," she whispered. "Please."

He shifted, taking a few steps toward the desk. He set her adorable ass on the wood top and nestled his head between her legs. He needed to bring her to the brink before he completely lost himself.

And it took only a few minutes before she was tugging at his hair. "Now, Jacob. I need you."

He stood, lifted her, and stumbled back to the bed. Rolling on top of her, he filled her, doing his best not to let his climax spill out immediately.

She lasted only a few minutes as her body convulsed and shivered. He followed seconds later.

It had proven to be an act of pure desire with only one end goal.

And they'd both gotten exactly what they needed.

He pulled her close to his body as he covered them with the warm comforter. He kissed her temple. "I love you." He lifted her hand and stared at the ring on her finger. "It suits you."

"I should take it off, but I'm too comfortable to get out of bed and put it safely back in its box." She glanced up. "I love you. I'm just not sure I'm ready for this yet."

"I know. But it's yours when you are. All you have to do is tell me."

She laughed. "We're so unconventional."

"Do you really want the bended-knee proposal?" he

asked.

"God, no. Nor do I want a church wedding. Hell, I'd be happy to get married in your front yard."

"Consider it done." He took her chin with his thumb and forefinger. "You're talking as if you might keep that ring on."

She held up her hand and wiggled her fingers. "That would be crazy."

"I don't think so." Looking at her hand, everything felt so right. Holding her in his arms, it was as if he'd finally come home. "But it's up to you. I've always told you that we don't even have to get married if you don't want to. As long as we're together, I don't care."

"Actually, you do." She kissed his chest and took in a deep breath, letting it out slowly. "And so does your family. To be honest, I like the idea, as well." She covered his mouth. "In the future."

He chuckled. "I'm on your timeframe, but there is something I think you should know."

"Now you're scaring me."

"I want to put in my notice when this case is over."

She bolted upright, keeping the sheet wrapped around her chest. It was a sexy look, and he couldn't stop himself from staring. "Why the hell would you do that?"

He blinked, trying to remember what he'd just said because the only thing he could focus on now was the sexy woman sitting in his bed. "Quit my job as a federal agent?"

"Yeah. That."

"Because the only reason I left the district attorney's office was to get out of Lake George so I could try to forget you. But that was hopeless."

"I thought you loved your job. Not to mention, you're kind of freaking awesome at it."

"I don't hate it, but I miss being in the courtroom. I just can't decide if I want to go back to the DA's office or maybe go work for my dad. He's always told me that I have a job if I want it."

"You want to defend criminals?" She arched a brow.

He laughed, tugging her back to his body. He held her tight. "No. But the look on your face was classic."

"Have you spoken to your old boss? Do you think the DA's office would even take you back?" She turned, tucking her back to his stomach.

"They offered me a job last week. I told them I needed time to think about it. However, I'm prepared to take it. What do you think?"

"I would love for you to work closer to home, but it's your career. Not mine. I'll support your decision, no matter what."

"Spoken like a true fiancée," he whispered, closing his eyes and letting his body relax. Even if she did take off the ring in the morning, they'd made peace with the past and had begun to mend their relationship, ensuring that the future would be filled with the kind of love he'd been dreaming of for the last few years.

10

*K*atie stood on the dock and stared at her house across the bay. She wrapped her arms around her middle. A cool summer breeze rolled in off the lake. Large puffy clouds floated across the morning sky, partially covering the sun, forcing the temperatures to remain colder than normal.

Boaters flocked to the lake in preparation for the holiday. The Fourth of July had always been one of the craziest weekends here, with tons of activity between the fireworks and massive parties in various locations. Katie always enjoyed sitting by the water and watching the night sky light up, but she never liked the crowds that came with the festivities.

She inhaled sharply, letting her lungs fill with the summer scents that reminded her of all the things she'd lost as a kid. The first few weeks after her mother had gone missing, she'd stayed with the Donovans. It had been bittersweet. Even though Jacob had been three years older, he'd always been her confidant. However, child protective services wouldn't let her stay in part because Raif was Owen's lawyer, and also because the Donovans weren't foster parents.

So, Katie had gone into the system and ended up living with a nice enough family in Saratoga. It wasn't the worst place to spend her youth, but her foster folks weren't her parents, and she'd never really bonded with them—though not for lack of trying on their part.

Or their other kids'.

Katie occasionally went back for visits, but it was always awkward. And, over time, she'd grown even more distant from those who'd done the best they could to love her when the world had turned out to be a cruel place. Perhaps she needed to visit them sooner rather than later and thank them properly for what they'd done for her. Because without them, she would have never survived the loneliness that she still had in her heart.

For twenty-seven years, she believed her mother had been murdered at the hands of her uncle.

The same man she'd believed had tried to kill her.

Owen had never adamantly denied it.

But he'd never admitted it, either.

The only thing he'd ever said was that he hoped she'd understand someday.

Well, hopefully, that day had come.

But she had more questions than answers, and

knowing that she was about to come face to face with her uncle, she wasn't sure she could face the truth.

"Katie. Owen is here," Jacob called from the house.

She glanced over her shoulder and waved. Never in a million years did she think she would take even five minutes out of her day to entertain a conversation with her uncle unless it meant him telling her where he'd hidden both her mother's body and the money he'd stolen. That's all she'd ever cared about, and those two things were still more important than anything else. But something told her that she was about to find out a whole lot more than she'd bargained for.

She pulled her sweater tighter as she made her way up the lawn to the patio where Raif, Isabelle, Jacob, and Owen were all standing, staring at her.

Jacob smiled, easing her growing unrest. She'd be lost without Jacob through all of this. When her uncle had been released from jail, Jacob had raced to be by her side. It didn't matter that she'd been treating him horribly. He'd known that she needed him, and he'd put up with her insults to do right by her—like always.

And then when Owen moved to Lake George, Jacob had moved in with her, giving her a lame excuse about wanting to be closer to his parents. She didn't care what his reasons were. She appreciated the gesture.

Besides, even if she couldn't admit it to herself, she needed Jacob. Outside of her business partner, Jacob was the only one who understood.

She rubbed her ring finger with her thumb. She'd

actually felt naked the second she'd taken off the engagement ring.

But she honestly wasn't ready to wear it. She and Jacob still had some things to work through. And they both needed some time to get used to the newness of being back together. It didn't matter the ease with which they had fallen back into their relationship; they had spent a few years apart, and Katie still had some questions about Hannah that she needed answered.

Only, last night hadn't been the right time or place for her to ask them.

Jacob stepped off the deck and closed the gap. "How are you holding up?" He wrapped his arm around her waist and kissed her cheek.

"About as well as can be expected." She leaned into him, drawing on this strength. "Has he said anything?"

"He's being quiet, waiting for you," Jacob said. "My mom brought out coffee, tea, and some muffins, trying to keep things normal."

"Your mom always thinks of everything. And if anyone can make this normal, she can."

"I've misunderstood her for years. It's something I need to fix. But that's for a different day."

Katie stepped up onto the deck and caught her uncle's gaze. "Hi," she said, for lack of anything better.

"You look good, Katie," Owen said, stretching out his hand as if they were meeting for the first time.

She took it in a polite shake but couldn't form any

words. She opened her mouth and tried. Twice. But nothing happened.

"Why don't we all take a seat?" Raif said.

Katie took the mug of hot, dark liquid that Jacob offered and sat so close to him, she might as well have been sitting on his lap.

He ran his hand up and down her thigh, squeezing every so often. He had a way of making her feel loved at precisely the right moment. Loving Jacob was the easy part. And letting go of the past proved to be simpler than she'd thought.

But she couldn't move forward until this chapter had closure. She needed that not only for her mother but also her own aching soul.

Everyone nibbled on a tasty baked treat and sipped their tea or coffee while the only noises were the birds chirping overhead and the boats humming up and down the shoreline.

Katie held her coffee mug and stared at the liquid as if it held all the answers. Five minutes ago, she'd been going over her list of questions. Right this second, she couldn't think of a single one.

"I can't take the silence," Jacob said. "So, let me cut to the chase." He reached across the coffee table and snagged a folder. He pulled out a picture of Edward.

Or Thurston.

Depending on if you asked Katie or Hannah.

"Do you know this man?" Jacob asked.

Owen took the image and studied it. "I can't say

that I do. Why? Who is he?" He glanced between Jacob and Katie with a straight face.

The Uncle Owen that Katie remembered from family photos always had a big smile. He seemed to love her in those pictures, always holding her hand, or she'd be sitting on his lap sharing some pie or as he drove the boat. They'd looked inseparable when she was a toddler.

But she had very few real memories of the man, and those she did, had come from seeing pictures of him while he was in prison.

He didn't have a smile on his face then. No. He'd hardened as a man, like most do when spending that much time in a maximum-security facility.

"He, as in Edward Howell, hired Katie to find his wife, MaryAnn Howell," Jacob said. "But he also approached Hannah as Thurston Howell, an FBI agent, which is bullshit. Do any of those names ring a bell with you?"

Owen narrowed his eyes. "Aside from the billionaire, his wife, and the rest of the castaways, where are you going with this?"

"Answer my question," Jacob said from behind a tight jaw.

Katie placed her hand over his and glanced at him. They both needed to keep their emotions in check.

"I will answer it after I know what you are thinking about this man and Katie's mother. I need to know, and you will understand."

Jacob shook his head. "I don't play games."

"That man does," Owen said, pointing to the picture. "Tell me your thoughts, and I'll fill in the blanks with what I know."

Katie cocked her head. "What the fuck does that mean?"

"It means I'm on your side," Owen said. "I always have been."

"I think MaryAnn is Grace." Jacob pulled out the picture that Edward had given Katie of his wife. He placed it on the table. Then he pulled out the one of Katie's mother that had been left at the house after the break-in.

Owen lifted both into his hands and squinted. "Where did you get this?" He waved at the one that had been left at the Bateman estate.

"I think my client broke into my house and left it for me," Katie said. "I have no pictures of my mom with blond hair."

"That's because she colored it," Owen whispered. "So, you now believe Grace is alive?"

"I do," Jacob said. "And I think you do, as well."

"Have you seen that man at all around town?" Raif asked.

Katie took Jacob's hand and squeezed.

"No. I haven't. But that doesn't surprise me. It's not me he cares about anymore. I can't hurt him, or so he thinks." Owen set the pictures on the table.

"What the hell does that mean?" Katie asked, tired of her uncle's vague answers.

"I'll get to that in a second," Owen said. "Why do you think my sister is still among the living?" He leaned back in his chair and folded his arms. It was almost as if he were daring Jacob in some kind of game.

"Cut the crap," Raif said. "You've been acting really weird lately, and it's pissing me off."

Owen nodded. "I was trying really hard not to put any of you in danger."

"From what?" Katie asked.

"Him." Owen pointed at the picture. "He's dangerous."

"I'm very confused. You say you don't know him, but then you go on about how he thinks you can't hurt him and say he's dangerous," Jacob said with a tight jaw. "So, which is it? Do you know him or not?"

"I don't know him." Owen tilted his head. "At least, not officially. But he's the man that Grace ran off with that night. He's the one who set me up, and he's the one who tried to kill Katie."

Katie gasped. "How do you know that if you've never met the man or can't remember what happened that night?"

"I'd like the answer to that question myself," Isabelle chimed in. "I've stood by my husband all these years. I've listened to the gossip and the bullshit that has nearly torn my family apart, all because you asked us to, and we gladly did so to protect Katie. But now you're being vague and dancing around so many important questions. I'm tired of it."

"So am I," Raif said. "So, please start talking, and stop with the excuses about doing all this to make sure nothing happens to us. We're all adults. Including my son and Katie. And if you haven't noticed, Jacob is a federal agent and—"

Owen held up his hand. "I'm well aware of what Jacob does for a living." He recrossed his legs as if he didn't have a care in the world. "You have to understand, I didn't have any real answers until a couple of days ago."

"What are you talking about?" Katie asked. "What changed in the last two days?"

"I've only had my speculations based on my sister's actions," Owen said. "And that started with her leaving you a couple of times the year before she disappeared. Something she never did."

"What do you mean by that?" Katie asked.

"She'd get a phone call and, all of a sudden, she had to go away for a week to take care of something. But she couldn't tell me what that was, and she couldn't take you." Owen let out a long breath. "I assumed it had to do with your birth father and him maybe trying to get back in your life, so I let it go. Maybe I shouldn't have."

"I feel like we're about to start talking in circles again," Jacob said. "Can you just be straight with us?"

"I'm trying to be, but you need to let me get there,

okay?" Owen rubbed the back of his neck. "I've also been looking for answers for as long as all of you have, only I had to do it from behind bars. Now that I have some, I need to be careful. Lives are at stake."

"Whose lives?" Isabelle asked.

"All of ours. But please, just let me get through this my way," Owen said.

"Go ahead," Katie said. "I want to hear everything."

Owen nodded. "I worried that Grace was off her meds the month or two before she disappeared. I did my best not to confront her about it because she never handled that well, but I wanted to make sure she was taking them. However, we ended up getting into a huge fight."

"I remember that," Isabelle said. "She called me, and we went out to lunch. She had a few choice words for you."

"I'm sure she did. She hated when she believed I was micromanaging her mental illness," Owen said. "However, I was so worried about her that I stooped to snooping, and that's when I found out that she'd taken out money from her personal account. When I confronted her, she went ballistic on me and told me that if I didn't stop meddling, she'd take Katie and leave forever. I couldn't have that, so I tried to drop it. Only the next thing I knew, I was being pulled from my car with handcuffs and being asked where I'd hidden the body."

"If you didn't know anything about what'd

happened to my mom, why did you give up on your defense and go to jail?"

Owen held up his finger. "I said I tried to let it go, but I couldn't. The night everything went down, I saw Grace packing. I asked her about it, and she told me that it was none of my business. I told her I wouldn't let her take Katie. That I knew she was off her meds. She told me I couldn't stop her."

"Jesus, Owen," Raif said. "You never told me any of this. Her being off her meds, her packing, all of this could have possibly helped your defense."

"I doubt that. There was no witness to this conversation, and it would only show how angry I was at Grace. I threatened her that night. I told I would do whatever it took to stop her from leaving. That including proving she was unfit to take care of Katie."

"You would have done that to Mom and me?" Katie swiped at her face.

"Yes," Owen said. "I know your mom loved you. That was never in question. But when she was full-on manic, she couldn't take care of you. I don't know if you remember her when she got like that or not, but it wasn't pretty. And I had to try to protect you." Owen glanced away. "I obviously failed."

"Was she manic the night she disappeared?"

Owen nodded. "She was all over the place, and when she tried to take her suitcase from her room and go downstairs, I grabbed her by the arm. She yanked free and screamed at me that I was hurting her and that it would leave a bruise. That if I tried to stop her again, she'd tell everyone that I abused her." He shook his head. "The reality is, I grabbed her hard enough that I did leave a mark."

"I can see how that wouldn't look good in front of a jury," Jacob said. "However, I'm really struggling with what all this has to do with present day and why you are here right now."

"You grew up to be a smart man," Owen said. "You're right. Grace and MaryAnn are the same woman."

Katie let out a guttural groan. "What does that make Edward or Thurston or whatever his name is?"

"He's your biological father, and Grace is terrified of him," Owen said.

"Is. As in present tense?" Isabelle asked. "Grace is alive?"

Katie took in a deep breath, letting it out slowly as Jacob rubbed her back. She blinked a few times but couldn't focus. "My mother is alive?"

"I couldn't believe it when she showed up on my doorstep a couple of days ago," Owen said.

"Fuck," Raif muttered. "Exactly how long have you known this?"

"Two days," Owen admitted.

Katie swallowed. Tears filled her eyes. "Where is she? Is she okay? What has she been doing all these years?"

Owen leaned forward. "She's with a friend of mine, and one of your friends is watching over them."

"Excuse me?" Katie blinked.

"I hired your friend Horace and someone I met on the inside to watch her so I could come here. She's not far away. I can call him and have her come here, but I fear Edward is watching this place," Owen said. "I've seen the news and have been following your case." He pointed at Jacob. "Grace believes with all her heart that her husband is a murderer. That he's the one who has been hunting those girls for the last twenty-seven years."

"Her husband, Edward, who is also my father, is possibly *The Doe Hunter*?" Katie swiped at her cheeks. "And she willingly left with him?" She shook her head. "Thank God, they stuffed me in a freezer," she mumbled.

"He lied to her," Owen said. "She didn't know what he'd done until years later. She honestly believed that I tried to kill Edward and her, and that I tried to harm Katie."

"But she stayed with him, even after she found out the truth, right?" Katie tried to rein in her anger, but it proved impossible.

"It's not that simple, Katie." Owen leaned forward. "She was gaslighted, and then eventually held hostage until she was able to gather enough evidence and money to leave him."

"Wait a second," Jacob said. "Edward told Katie that

his wife had taken something from him. Do you know what that is?"

Owen nodded. "Proof that he stole the money that is rightfully Katie's. Edward told Grace that Owen made it impossible for Grace to get a dime, except he'd managed to steal it all—oddly, with her help."

"How is that possible?" Katie asked.

"She believed Edward was rich, but he wasn't. He was a washed-up gambler and hustler, who stole all your money and made it look like I killed your mom. When she and Edward left, she'd been shot a few different times. She thought I had done it."

"What? Why did she believe that?" Isabelle asked.

"Because the man who actually shot her was wearing a mask," Owen said. "After our fight, I went downstairs to calm down and had a glass of wine from a bottle that was already open. I hadn't remembered opening it, but since only a small glass was missing, I didn't think anything of it. I drank some, and that's the last thing I remember."

"And my mom? What happened to her?" Katie asked.

"Someone came upstairs and shot her," Owen said.

"And you know all this because Grace told you?" Isabelle asked. "I'd sure like to hear this from the horse's mouth."

"Don't be mad at her," Owen said. "She's been living in a different kind of hell than the rest of us."

Katie stood and turned to face the lake. For twenty-seven years, she'd believed her mother had been murdered. "How long has my mother been in this area?"

"About two months," Owen said. "She's been living in one rundown hotel after the other between Glens Falls and Ticonderoga. She never thought he'd come looking for her here."

Katie blinked away a couple of tears. "And she never thought to contact me?"

"It wasn't that simple," Owen said. "If her husband showed up, she didn't want to put you in danger—which is exactly what happened."

"Then why did she come back?" Raif asked.

"She came here to get a glimpse of you. To make sure you were okay. And then she planned on leaving, but Edward showed up, and she got scared."

Katie turned on her heels. "So, what you're saying is that she never intended to turn him in? Or come to Raif to tell him what she knew? She had no intention of clearing your name?"

"She's scared, Katie. He's a monster, and he'd kill any of us and not think twice. What she stole is her leverage over him, and what she believed would keep you alive." Owen stood and inched closer. "She planned on using it to blackmail him to keep his distance from you, Jacob, and his family."

Katie held up her hand and, thankfully, Jacob stood, wrapping his arm around her waist, holding her steady. She knew she shouldn't hold this much resentment for a woman who had been dead to her for nearly three decades, but she couldn't help it. So many lies were wrapped up in her family legacy, it made her sick to her stomach. "When did she find out my father was a serial killer?"

"I'm not exactly sure. Sometime in the last five years or so," Owen said. "Your mother spent much of the last twenty-something years drinking herself to the point where she doesn't remember much of her life. She numbed herself to reality."

"That's no excuse," Raif said. "If she knew, she had choices."

"Edward had her believing that he always had eyes on Katie and that he'd kill her the second Grace betrayed him. It wasn't until she had proof of the kind of monster he was and had access to some money that she felt comfortable enough to leave."

"So, he knows what she has," Jacob said as more of a statement than a question.

"Oh, he knows," Owen said. "That's what brought him here. And for the record, Grace doesn't believe he came to Lake George because he believes she came back here, but because he wants to use Katie to somehow get to Grace."

"Wait a second," Raif said. "You don't think he knows Grace is here?"

"If he did, he'd take her, and they'd be gone. Or Grace would be dead."

"Okay," Katie asked. "But if he's here for me, then why am I still breathing?" Katie asked.

"Because you have a federal agent living you," Owen said. "And who knows exactly what kind of game he's playing. Edward never killed Grace because, in his twisted mind, he thinks he loves her. And he knows you're his kid, so maybe his end game isn't to kill you."

Jacob shook his head. "That might have been his thought in the beginning, but back that kind of animal into a corner, and he'll do whatever he has to in order to survive—even kill his own."

"I agree. That's why I'm here telling you all this," Owen said.

"Shit." Raif folded his arms. "Are you telling me that you would have kept this from me? From Katie?"

"Yes," Owen said. "If it meant keeping my sister and niece alive, you can bet your last dollar I would have kept it from you."

"You have a fucking death wish," Raif mumbled.

"No. He doesn't." Jacob kissed Katie's temple. "I don't agree with what he's done, but if Edward is my serial killer, which I believe he is, I would have done the same thing as Owen did."

"Thank you," Owen said.

"I wouldn't thank me." Jacob squeezed Katie's waist. "You're going to have to take me to Grace so I can set her up in a safe house. I need to interview her. And you. Officially."

"I don't like the sound of that, and neither will she."

Owen leaned back. "But I'll do whatever you need me to do. I want this to be over, and I want my sister and niece back."

Katie glanced at Jacob. "I want to talk with her. I want to see her."

Jacob nodded. "I'll make sure that happens. But not until I know she's in a safe place, and that asshole isn't following us."

"I can live with that." She rubbed her temples. "I can't believe my mother is alive."

"Believe it," Owen said. "But understand that she's not only scared of Edward, she's also terrified that you won't like her or forgive her for what she's done."

Katie didn't want to admit this out loud, but that was a distinct possibility. "Right now, the focus needs to be on catching Edward. We'll deal with the rest later."

11

Katie blew out a puff of air and tilted her head toward the ceiling of Jacob's beat-up old truck.

"Are you sure you're ready for this?" Jacob reached across the front seat and rubbed the back of her neck tenderly.

"I have no idea. Every scenario I've ever played out in my head when it comes to finding my mother has always been about having a proper funeral for her, not having a conversation with a woman I've mourned for decades."

Jacob pulled her closer, giving her a quick, sweet kiss. "It's okay to be mad at her."

"I know," Katie said. "It's just that I had this image of her in my head, and it's not the portrait my uncle paints."

"And he's not what you remember, either."

"No. He's not." Katie pressed her forehead against Jacob's and closed her eyes for a brief moment. "Thank you for being here with me."

"Of course," he whispered. "Are you sure you don't want me to go inside with you?"

She blinked. "I need to see her alone."

"Okay. Cameron and I will be right outside if you need either of us, okay?"

She brushed her lips over his and held him for a long moment. "I love you," she whispered.

"I love you more."

Katie stepped from the SUV and rubbed her hands over the top of her jeans. She adjusted her ponytail before snagging her Jets cap and tugging her hair through the hole in the back.

Her heels clicked on the sidewalk as she made her way toward the front door of a house on the outskirts of the village. Jacob's partner, Cameron, stood at attention by the front door.

"You must be Katie," Cameron said.

"And you must be the boy genius."

Cameron laughed. "I hate it when he calls me that."

"It's a compliment, and he's used to being the smartest person in most rooms, so when he meets someone that is not only smarter but also challenges him, he likes to razz them a bit. He doesn't give out nicknames often."

"His old partner said he's only given out one other."

Katie laughed. "To Stacey, a state trooper. He calls her Watson."

"Why not Sherlock?"

"He thinks Watson is smarter."

"Are you sure it's not because Jacob thinks he's Sherlock," Cameron said as he opened the door.

Katie cocked her head. "Why, boy genius, you might be correct in your assessment." Her heart dropped to her gut the second she stepped into the small living room. A woman sat in the corner on a wingback chair with her legs up on an ottoman. She sipped on what looked like a glass of sweet tea while reading a book.

Her hair was blond, but her roots were coming in grey with some red woven in. She glanced up, and her jaw slackened. "Katie," she whispered. "Is that you?" She set her things on the table next to the chair and stood.

Katie opened her mouth but wasn't sure if she should call the woman Grace, MaryAnn, or Mom. She cleared her throat. "Hi," she said, opting not to commit to anything just yet.

"I'm glad you came," Grace said, waving her hand at the sofa. On the coffee table was a tray with a pitcher of tea, another glass, and a plate of cookies.

Snickerdoodles, to be exact.

Katie's favorite.

She took a seat on the sofa and folded her hands in her lap. "We don't have much time before Jacob's team gets here to question you."

"I don't understand why he can't do it." Grace eased

back in the chair, pushing the ottoman aside. She crossed her feet at the ankles and sat up tall as if she were some kind of Southern belle. "He seems like a nice young man."

"He is, but being Raif's son, he can't be involved in the case anymore."

"What about his partner?"

"They are letting him stay on as a consultant, but he's too close to Jacob," Katie said. "Why are you so interested in who is heading up the investigation?"

"Just like you don't trust me, I don't trust that anyone can keep me safe from Edward. When he finds me, he'll make me pay for what I did. I just hope it's not the way he's threatened."

"What did he say he'd do?"

Grace recrossed her ankles. "When I found out what he was doing on his hunting trips, I tried to leave. I packed my bags and left on the second night he'd been away. I got as far as LA, but he had a tracker on my phone, and I didn't know it. He showed me pictures of you with Jacob. It was five and a half years ago, but I remember it like it was yesterday because I couldn't believe he'd had someone watching you all these years."

Katie hugged herself and shivered.

"He told me if I ever left again, he'd kill you the same way he'd killed those girls."

"You left a second time. Why did you take the risk?" Katie asked. "You know why. I have all those girls' drivers' licenses and a couple of his journals that document his hunts. I gave them to the FBI, along with some documentation about the foundation."

"You gave the feds enough to issue a warrant for Edward's arrest."

"I also have about two million in cash that belongs to you," Grace said.

Katie laughed. "Not really. It's evidence."

"And after they catch and convict Edward?"

"Then it will go back to the foundation first. My personal money will be the last that gets returned." Katie leaned forward and poured some tea.

"That doesn't seem fair."

"That's the way it works." Nothing about Katie's life had been fair, but the world didn't work that way, and she'd always managed to land on her feet.

This would be no different.

Especially now that Jacob was back in her life.

Katie chugged half her drink. She wiped her lips with the back of her hand. "Why didn't you take me with you?"

"In my mind, that was always the plan, but I don't think your father—"

"He might be that biologically, but don't ever call him that again." Katie tried to take a deep breath, but she couldn't fill her lungs. Rage, however, engulfed her heart and soul.

Grace nodded. "Edward never had any intention of bringing you with us. Had I known that, I wouldn't have gone along with any of it, but he had a way of making me believe everything he said. He really can be charming when he wants to be."

Bile smacked the back of Katie's throat. "Don't make excuses for him. Or you. Just answer my questions." She wondered if she was being too hard on her mother. Jacob had warned her about her swirling emotions and not letting too many of them hit the surface.

She needed to keep her professional hat on, but that proved impossible at the moment.

"I packed a bag for you, but I have no idea what happened to it. I woke up after someone shot me."

"Who?"

"Edward told me it was Owen, but whoever it was, he wore a mask."

"You honestly believed your own brother would have shot you while you are sleeping?" Katie asked.

"You believed he murdered me for most of your life." Grace folded her arms.

"Fair enough," Katie said.

"Please understand, I was off my medication. When that happens, I'm not in my right mind. I thought Edward was the love of my life, and he told me that Owen had set it up to make it look like I tried to kill him."

"That makes no sense at all if he was the one shooting you."

Grace nodded. "Edward came up with this elaborate story. At the time, it made sense. And when he showed me that Owen had gone to jail for killing me, he told me that our little girl would be forever safe in her new home and that we could live out our lives in Vegas. But I missed you so much, I couldn't stand myself. I refused my meds and drank, and Edward did whatever it was that Edward did."

"Are you taking your medication now?" Katie asked.

Grace nodded. "I've been on them regularly for the last three years."

"You fit Edward's type. Why hasn't he killed you?"

"When I first met him, he asked me if I wanted to go camping with him, and I said unless his idea of camping was at a hotel, the answer was no."

"Were you living at home then?"

Grace shook her head. "I was in New York City, and Edward had to be the most gorgeous, charming man I'd ever met. But I seriously have always hated camping. No amount of charm could make me go, not even after I slept with him. So, off he went, and I didn't see him again for three months until he waltzed back into the hotel I'd been staying at, and I informed him that I was pregnant with you."

"That must have been quite the shock."

"It was, and he didn't believe me at first. I told him I didn't need him to raise my baby, and he seemed to be fine with that. But then he changed his mind."

"Why didn't he come back to Lake George with you?"

"Your grandfather was dying, and I wanted him to

meet you. But that didn't go too well. He was so disappointed in me that he told me he was cutting me from the will."

"I don't remember Granddad at all."

"He could be a mean old man sometimes, and he was the only family member to meet Edward, though back then, he went by his first name, Thurston. Grandpa told me that he thought Edward was a snake, and that if I stayed with him, I could kiss my money and the house goodbye. Edward told me not to worry. Said he would stay in the background. He said he could be patient, but my dad died a day later."

Katie gasped. "Do you think Edward killed him?"

"I do now," Grace admitted.

"I was two when Granddad died. You didn't leave for another two years. What was Edward doing during that time?"

"He said he was making sure we would have a good life. He earned his money gambling, and he was trying to go legit. He told me he got a job as a manager of a casino in Vegas, but that it would take some time for us to have a big enough nest egg for him to take care of me without having to rely on the money, which was now tied up with the foundation, you, and Owen."

"But if Granddad died so quickly, he couldn't have had a chance to change his will."

Grace laughed. "It was always set up to skip Owen and me if there were grandchildren involved. I didn't know that. Like I said, my father could be cruel, so he was just playing with me. I was already out, but you weren't. You stood to inherit it all. But Edward manipulated the foundation and stole the money, leaving you with almost nothing."

"And the inability to sell the house," Katie mumbled. "Not that I want to sell it, but you and Edward have both caused me and Uncle Owen a great deal of pain."

"Owen brought some on himself by not telling the truth about what he knew."

"He knew almost nothing. He was drugged and set up." Katie swallowed. Her heart thumped in her throat. Owen had sacrificed everything.

"Only he lied about one very important detail, and he continues to lie about it."

Katie leaned forward. "What's that?"

"He has met Edward. He must have. Because it's his signature on the paperwork with the foundation that put all that money in Edward's pocket."

*Jacob leaned against the hood of his car, waiting for Cameron to complete his perimeter check. If Edward were a smart man, he would be long gone.

Well, Jacob knew the asshole was smart, the question was how cocky he was and how much did he really want to fuck with Katie.

Or kill her.

Every murderer had a code they lived by. It sounded odd, but without rules, killers were chaotic, and Edward was definitely methodical.

"All clear," Cameron said as he adjusted his weapon on his side holster. "It has to be killing you to take a back seat on this case."

"Not really," Jacob admitted. "You should probably know that I'm going to be leaving the FBI."

"You've got to be fucking kidding me." Cameron planted his hands on his hips. "Why?"

"I miss being a lawyer and being in court. I only took this job to run away from my mistakes. Now that I've corrected them, apologized, and I have Katie back, I realized this is not how I want to deal with the bad guys of the world."

"Well, that fucking sucks for me." Cameron leaned against the front of the SUV next to Jacob and folded his arms. "I really like working with you. I admire and respect you."

"I feel the same way," Jacob said. "You're an excellent agent. I'll make a recommendation for a new partner. I think you'd work well with Toby."

"He wouldn't be horrible." Cameron nodded as he pulled out his cell. "This is Agent Thatcher."

Jacob pushed from his truck and took a few steps forward. He wished he could see inside the windows, but the curtains were drawn shut.

"I've got to take a waltz down the street," Cameron said. "A woman reported she might have seen someone lurking in the back alley behind her house and she's spooked with two federal agents hanging out in the street."

"I've got eyes on the house," Jacob said.

"I won't be but ten minutes or so. I'll make sure to do a check on the way back, so just stay out front."

Jacob nodded. He inched closer to the front door, glancing up and down the street, keeping his hands on his weapon, he continued to ease closer. All of a sudden, a chill crept across his skin. Something didn't sit right with this, and Jacob always trusted his gut.

The sound of a twig snapping caught his attention. He gripped the butt of his gun and turned on his heels.

Something came down hard and fast on his temple.

He groaned and dropped to his knees. His vision blurred. He blinked as liquid trickled down the side of his face.

"Edward?"

A siren rang out in the distance.

Edward raised his weapon, and a sharp pain landed right on the top of Jacob's head before the world went dark.

"How do you know that Owen has met Edward?" Katie asked. She was so sick of lies and betrayal. She still didn't completely trust her uncle, but she sure as shit didn't trust her mother.

"Because Edward told me."

"Seriously? And Edward's word is good enough for you?" Katie did her best not to burst out laughing. She didn't want to completely insult Grace because she needed to continue to extract as much information as she could so they could find Edward and make sure he spent the rest of his life rotting in prison.

"He had pictures of them together," Grace said. "Sitting at the Antlers, drinking and smoking cigars. They looked as though they were laughing and having a good time. I took those pictures."

"You gave them to the feds?" Katie leaned forward.

Grace shook her head.

"Why not?"

"I didn't think it was important," Grace said. "It only proved to me that Owen was trying to steal all the money for himself, which Owen says isn't true."

"Has he seen the pictures?"

"He says they're fake. That Edward must have had them photoshopped because he's never met him. But I don't know if I believe that. In order for Edward to get the money, he had to have Owen's signature. And he got that. Mine was easy, he had me sign papers all the time, and I was so trusting, I never looked at them."

"Can I see the pictures?" Katie had remembered that during the trial, the signatures had been authenticated. It had been some damning evidence against her uncle, and something he didn't deny during the actual trial, though he had to Raif.

And he had earlier in the day.

But he hadn't said anything about the pictures.

"Sure." Grace stood and strolled into the kitchen. She'd aged a lot from the images that Katie had from when she was little. More so than Katie thought a woman of fifty-nine should have. Grace returned with a small bag and pulled out a folder. "Here they are."

Katie took the copies and glanced at them. They looked real enough, but that didn't mean anything. "Do you have more copies?"

"No," Grace said. "Edward is a lot of things, but—"

"He's a murderer," Katie said. "A serial killer who has probably killed more people than any other killer in the history of this country." She handed the pictures back. "If Owen said he never met Edward, I believe him."

"How else do explain the signatures? It's not that easy to forge—"

"It's easier than you think." Katie pinched the bridge of her nose. "Do you still love him?"

Grace sat back down in the corner chair. "He's all I've ever known. It wasn't easy to leave him. He took care of me when I refused to take my meds. He never left my side, and trust me, I can be a lot to handle."

"Are you kidding me?"

"I know that sounds crazy, but I thought he was protecting you all these years. When I found out otherwise, that's when I knew I needed to leave. I couldn't do that until I had gathered enough to hold it over his head, so he'd never do anything to me. Or to you."

"But you had no intention of turning him in or being reunited with me."

Grace took a tissue and dabbed at her eyes. "I've lived without you since you were four years old. I figured you were better off without me. Not to mention, if I came back from the dead, he'd know it."

Her mother had a point. A good one.

The sound of something hitting the pavement outside caught her attention. She spun on her heels, snagging her weapon from its holster.

"What's wrong?" Grace asked.

Did you hear—?

Crash!

Bang!

Grace screamed as she grabbed her shoulder.

"Mom!" Katie glanced between her mother and the assailant, who'd shot Grace in the shoulder. "Edward," she said from between gritted teeth.

"You're not going to call me *Dad*?" Edward held his gun to Katie's face. "I'd drop that, or I will shoot." He changed his aim back to Grace. "And this time, I'll kill her. I don't think you want that."

Katie held her weapon high. "Where are Jacob and Cameron?"

"Bleeding out somewhere," Edward said with a smile and gathered up a stack of paperwork and

Grace's bag. "Now, give me your weapon. We need to leave."

Katie glanced at Grace, who had slumped in the chair, holding her shoulder.

Katie took her finger off the trigger and handed Edward her weapon. With her cell tucked into her back pocket, Jacob would be able to track her cell.

"That's my good girl." Edward put the gun in his pants. "Where's your phone?" He pushed her toward the back of the house.

"I left it in the—"

"Don't lie to me." He turned her around, harshly, and pulled it from her pocket. He tossed it to the floor and yanked her by the ponytail. "We'd better get a move on." He opened the back door and shoved her outside.

She stumbled down the pathway. "Those sirens sound close."

"About a mile away." Edward laughed. "But I accounted for that." He pushed open the back door and in the alley was what looked like an undercover police car. "It's stolen, but I doubt it's been reported yet since the cop is unconscious." He waved his weapon at the driver's side. "You're driving."

Katie swallowed. Hard. "Where are we going?"

"To the site of my very first hunt. I think it's time to relive that thrill."

12

"I'm fine." Jacob rubbed the back of his neck, only it was the top of his head that throbbed.

"Agent Donovan—"

"Edge, I've known you my entire life. I think you can call me by my first name." Jacob stared at his longtime friend and paramedic.

"Sorry," Edge said. "You were knocked out for a good ten minutes. I really think you should go to the hospital."

"I agree," Jackson said as he approached the ambulance.

"You know that's not going to happen. Not when my girlfriend is missing, and I'm shocked you, of all people, would want me to go." Jacob pointed to Jackson.

"I didn't say that. I just agreed that it might be a

good idea." Jackson shook his hand. "What the fuck happened?"

"Bastard has Katie." Bile smacked the back of Jacob's throat. "He set up a diversion to separate Cameron and me and moved in quickly. Normally, I'd track her cell, but she left it behind."

"Or he made her leave it, which is more likely," Jackson said. "Katie doesn't go anywhere without it."

"That's true," Jacob said.

Rochelle and Renee, two other paramedics, rolled Grace out on a gurney. Following them was Jared and one of his other troopers, Tristan.

Jacob raced toward the troopers.

"I wasn't done with you," Edge called.

Jacob ignored him. "What did she have to say?"

"Nothing different than what you told us," Jared said.

Jacob eyed Cameron, hobbling up the street. He waved. Cameron moved a little faster.

"Will either of you go to the hospital and get checked out?" Tristan asked.

"And if it was Brooke who had been abducted, would you go?" Jacob asked.

"Fuck, no," Tristan admitted. "Here comes Edge. And he doesn't look happy."

"I want you to either see a doctor in a day or two or come to the station house and let me check you out. Got it?" Edge glared.

Jacob nodded as he made his way to Grace's gurney. "How is she?"

"Bullet went all the way through," Renee said. "She lost a fair amount of blood, but she's going to be fine."

Grace reached out with her good arm and grabbed Jacob's hand. "Find my little girl, please."

"That's the plan," Jacob said. "Do you have any idea where he might have taken her?"

"I wish I knew," Grace said. "I had no idea he knew this area. When I met him, he said he'd never been here, but I've since learned that's not true."

Jacob pulled out his card. "If you think of anything at all, call me, okay?"

"He took all my files. All the evidence I had tying him to those murdered girls." A few tears rolled down Grace's cheek.

"Cameron left them in the house?"

Grace nodded. "I've screwed up so many things, and I wish I had done this differently. I wish I had gone right to the police when I found the evidence."

Jacob squeezed her hand. "I'm going to find Katie. Don't you worry." And he would find out why the fuck Cameron had left something so valuable inside.

"I'm sorry," Grace said through a guttural sob. "I'm so, so sorry."

Renee and Rochelle lifted the gurney into the ambulance.

"We need to get rolling," Renee said. "We'll be in touch."

"Thanks," Jacob said just as Cameron joined the party.

He shook everyone's hand. "The sheriff that had his car stolen was shot in the side. The bullet missed all of his important organs. He said Edward aimed there. Why would he do that?"

"Because he didn't want to kill him for some reason. Which sort of doesn't make sense. It's a witness. Jacob ran a hand over his head. "I need to talk to you about something. Privately."

Cameron blew out a puff of air. "You want to know about the box of evidence, right?"

Jacob glanced between Jared and Tristan and then back to Cameron.

"I don't mind saying this in front of them," Cameron said. "Our boss told me to do it. Other than the licenses, it's all copies of the originals."

"What the fuck, Cameron? Why? Did you just use my girlfriend and her mother as bait and neglect to tell me?"

"Not really." Cameron stuffed his hands into his pockets. "I was following orders. The good news is that there is a tracking device in the box. We've already got a bead on them. They are headed north on 87. A car's headed that way."

"Then so am I. And you're going to keep feeding me those coordinates."

Cameron nodded. "But we should talk about Veronica Hemmings."

"Who is she?" Tristan asked.

"Jesus. I vaguely remember that name and case," Jared said. "She was murdered up in the Adirondacks. Her killer was never found, but it was believed that it was her boyfriend."

"There is no way the boyfriend killed Veronica," Cameron said. "We believe it might have been *The Doe Hunter's* very first victim. And we have at least two other victims from that timeframe that were murdered in upstate New York that we believe could have been him."

"And all of that happened right before Grace disappeared." Jacob rubbed the back of his neck again in hopes of helping his throbbing headache. He rocked back and forth. "I need to get the fuck out of here."

"I know, but they only have a half-hour jump, and we have a car. Let's talk some of this through before you go off half-cocked."

"One of my troopers used to be a Ranger," Jared said. "You know Morgan."

Jacob nodded.

"I'll have him contact some buddies. They can start to be on the lookout," Jared said.

"I appreciate that." Jacob let out a long breath.

Cameron waved his phone. "The boss is keeping me on the case, so he's sending a car for me."

"That's good news," Jacob said.

"Sort of. He wants me in the office, working intel," Cameron said.

"That's better than nothing." Jacob glanced around. The crime scene unit had arrived and were unpacking their equipment and heading inside the safe house. "Besides, you're smarter than anyone in that office, and I'd feel better if you were the one staying in his mind and directing traffic, so to speak. Now, I need to go."

Cameron nodded. "I told them you were going to the hospital. They don't want you anywhere near this case, and my ride is ten minutes out."

"That doesn't surprise me," Jacob said.

"Be careful out there. Edward might be going back to where it all began, but this is uncharted waters for him," Cameron said.

"What do you mean?" Tristan said.

"I've been thinking about what his code might be, and since he's never killed Grace and he left Katie behind, I imagine killing family, or at least people he's supposed to care about, might be hard. And he didn't kill Owen or Jacob."

"Neither of us is family," Jacob said.

"But you are to Grace and Katie." Cameron arched a brow. "And he didn't kill me or the sheriff. As a matter of fact, it's as if he went out of his way not to. We found out that his father was a cop, and his mother was a first responder."

"That's interesting, but he took Katie. I would think that means he's going to kill her," Jacob said.

Cameron nodded. "That's why he's going back to where it all began. Now, get going."

"I'm going with Jacob," Jackson said.

"I'm not going to say no." Jacob slapped Jackson on the back.

"Tristan and I are going to pretend we didn't hear that," Jared said. "Call me if you need me, though."

"Stay in touch." Jacob nodded toward Jackson's SUV. "You're driving."

"Of course, I am. If we took your car, everyone and their mother would know we were coming."

The clock was ticking, and he knew they didn't have much time. "Cameron, where is she now?"

"Still on the Northway between Schroon Falls and North Hudson. My guess is they are headed to the trail off Route 9 and then south to follow Bouquet River. Veronica was found not far from the South Fork campsites."

Jacob jogged down the street and climbed into the passenger side of Jackson's vehicle. "I hope you've learned to drive like Katie."

"Only when my family isn't in the car. So buckle up and hold on."

Katie stepped from the vehicle and stretched out her back while Edward stuffed some things from the box of evidence into a bag that held his weapons. "What are we doing here?" She hadn't been hiking in the Adirondacks since the last time she'd gone with Jacob, though they hadn't ever started from this point.

"I'm reminiscing about the first time I realized what kind of person I am." He zipped up the satchel.

"You mean a psychopath?" she mumbled.

He gave her a good shove toward the trail. "Is that any way to speak to your father?"

"Sperm donation doesn't make you a dad."

He laughed.

"Does your mother hosting you in her uterus make her a mom?"

"Not one bit." She waved her hand as she stepped into a swarm of gnats. "So, what did you do up here and when?"

"I killed my first victim, sort of."

"What the hell does that mean?" She did her best not to glance over her shoulder, though she couldn't stand that he was two paces behind her, knowing that he had a gun pointed at her back.

"I didn't get to actually shoot her with my bow."

"Aw, too bad for you."

Edward grabbed her by the ponytail and yanked her backward.

She groaned as she stumbled, her hands flapping as she tried to find her hair and stop the pain. "Fuck."

"You have a nasty mouth. I'd stop if I were you." He shoved her forward, and she fell to her knees. "Get up."

She jumped to her feet, brushed the dirt off, and then continued walking on the trail as she scratched her head. He must have pulled out a whole handful of her hair.

"How did she die if you didn't shoot her?"

"I read in the papers that some other hikers found her near death. They brought her to the hospital, but it was too late. She died from some internal injuries and dehydration."

"Did you beat her?"

"No. But I had been hunting her for five days. She was a smart one, that girl. I did manage to stab her a couple of times, but she kept on running. I have to say, she was one of the most exhilarating kills I've ever experienced." He curled his fingers around her biceps and tugged her off the trail. "I learned so much from her and I never made those mistakes again."

"Is that what you plan to do with me? Hunt me?"

"I didn't want to kill you, but your mother has left me with no choice."

"You always have a choice. And I've got news for you, I'm not going to run. I'm not going to let you hunt me like an animal."

Edward laughed. "Yes, you are. Because if you don't, I'll find another person on this trail, and I'll kill them."

"You wouldn't. It goes against what defines you as a killer."

"I've already done that. I had to kill a boyfriend because he got in the way. I've had to kill without really hunting. I've had to adjust my hunger and be as satisfied as I can."

"And how is that working out for you?" She turned and caught his menacing glare.

He shrugged. "It has its moments, like this one."

"Killing your own daughter excites you?"

He had the nerve to frown. "I can't say that it does."

All she had to do was keep Edward talking. Maybe, just maybe, that would give her time to come up with an escape plan. Because she knew without a doubt that if she let him hunt her, she'd probably lose. She didn't know the area, and she would bet her last dollar that he'd been studying this trail and its surrounding woods.

Not only that, even though he was hunting with a bow and arrow, he still had decent range. He wouldn't have to show himself to kill her. She also didn't know how much of a head start he would give her. And if he stripped her naked, which is what it appeared he did to all his victims, it would hinder a woman's ability to run simply because she'd feel even more exposed and vulnerable.

Especially in broad daylight.

"You won't get away with this," she said. "Everyone knows who you are now."

"They can't prove it. There is no DNA evidence that links me to any of the murders."

"Grace gave proof to the FBI."

Edward paused mid-step. "I took all that back," he said.

"You don't look too sure of yourself," Katie said. "I

mean, did you really think the FBI would leave all that evidence in a safe house unattended? I'm sure what you have is copies."

He laughed. "Maybe your boyfriend isn't as smart as you think he is. Because in that box were what they call my trophies."

Katie swallowed. No way would Cameron have done that unless he'd had a plan. Only, what kind of plan left her as bait without telling her?

She shivered as she sidestepped a few large, low-hanging branches. She zigzagged through the woods, still heading mostly south, but a little west from the designated path. Every time she went too far in one direction, Edward corrected her, so he definitely had a specific spot in mind.

Which meant he had a plan for his hunting pattern.

"You can stop now," Edward commanded.

She turned and stared him in the eye. All she saw was a monster. There was no humanity staring back at her, and that alone was terrifying. Not just because he'd pulled out his bow and was adjusting his arrow pack on his shoulder, but because his DNA had helped to create a child. His blood ran through *her* body.

Add in the mental illness that had plagued her mother, and Katie wondered how those genes had managed to escape her make-up. What if she had children, and those horrific traits made their way to her offspring?

Shit. This wasn't the time or place to be thinking

about her future. Because at this rate, she wasn't going to have one to worry about.

"If you think I'm going to strip and run like a wild animal so you can get your rocks off, you're even crazier than I thought."

He laughed. "You're my daughter. I'm not going to make you take your clothes off. That would really be disturbing, now, wouldn't it?" he said with a sarcastic laugh.

"And hunting me down like a wild boar isn't?"

"I didn't want to have to do this, but your mother, you, and everyone else in your world has left me with no other choice."

"If your plan wasn't to kill me all along, then what was it?" She found a rock and sat on it, digging her heels into the ground. There was no way she was running. If she were going to die, he would have to kill her while looking her in the eye. *Let's see if the coward has the balls to do that.* "Did you really want me to find my mother?"

"No. I didn't believe she was stupid enough to come here and stay in the area for any length of time," Edward said, leaning against a tree.

"Then why did you come to my office? Why did you break into my home and vandalize it and leave me a picture of my mother?"

"I wanted to see what you were like. Looking at you from a distance wasn't enough. So, I came up with a story." He smiled. "The rest was simply trying to fuck with Owen and make him look bad."

"Why use a real picture of Grace? You had to have known I would notice the resemblance."

He smiled. "I wanted to see your reaction, but you're good at keeping them close to the vest. I was impressed." He took out an arrow and waved it in front of her. "Time to get up and get on the move. I will give you fifteen minutes."

"That's not much of a head start."

He shrugged. "We don't have much time."

"Well, you might as well shoot me now because I told you, I'm not letting you hunt me down." She folded her arms like a defiant child.

"Don't anger me," he said behind a tight jaw. "See that couple over there, taking a break on the trail?"

She turned her head, and her heart dropped to her gut. "Yes," she said softly.

"If you don't get up and start running, I'll shoot them." He held his arrow up to his bow. "And if you head toward the trail, I'll kill the first person I see."

She glanced around. The area was pretty open, so when she started running, she didn't have any place to hide for a long while. "I turn and run, and you're going to shoot me in the back in five minutes."

"Maybe," he said with a snarl. "But would you rather me kill them over there?"

In her head, she calculated the time from when the sirens were only a few minutes out, how long it took them to get to the parking area—which, for her, she'd driven painfully slow—and the time it had taken them to get to this particular spot.

It was possible that the police, if they knew where Edward was headed, could be at the parking lot by now. Which meant they were half an hour away.

Of course, she had to believe there was a reason they'd left that box of goodies in that house. Which meant maybe she was being watched right now.

She pushed herself to a standing position and brushed her hands over her jeans. "You're a bastard," she said. "And I hope you rot in hell." She adjusted her ponytail and turned. A tingle crawled up her spine. She shivered as she took a few steps west. Restraining the urge to take off running, she initially kept her pace at a brisk walk.

This was not how she'd planned on dying, and she'd be damned if she let Edward win at this game.

Jacob adjusted his earpiece and kept his weapon at the ready. The woods were crawling with federal agents, troopers, rangers, and other first responders. They were able to clear the area before Edward and Katie were seen getting out of the stolen undercover vehicle.

Jackson and Jacob had pulled in only a half-hour after Katie had parked the vehicle. It must have killed her to drive the fucking speed limit. Jacob had to wonder if Edward had made her do that so as not to draw attention, though he had to know that everyone would be looking for that damn cop car.

However, it appeared that he had no idea there'd been a tracking device.

"He took the licenses and the documents tying him to the foundation," Jackson said. "But he left the rest."

"That means he probably has another car stashed somewhere." Jacob crossed the street and moved onto the main hiking path.

"Do you really think he's going to follow the trail?" Jackson asked.

"No." Jacob touched his earpiece that Cameron had hooked him up with. "But someone must have—" The crackle of the communication device buzzed in his ear. He paused.

"We've got eyes on both Edward and Katie," someone said. "Fifty feet off the trail about one mile in."

"Let's go." Jacob took off at a jog, flanking the woods.

"I don't have an earpiece, so you need to tell me what the fuck is going on." Jackson was one pace behind him.

"They have a lock on both Edward and Katie. He's starting the hunting game."

"Fuck," Jackson muttered. "Are they in position to take him out?"

"Almost." Jacob ran as fast as he could, listening to

the chatter in his ear, trying to gauge where he was going. He pointed toward the trail, hoping Jackson understood.

He nodded and took off running alongside the trail.

Jacob kept him in his sights, but he needed to head west about fifty feet beyond the trail. That's what the agent in his ear had calculated for where Edward and Katie were moving.

"Jacob, I can see you," the voice said. "You're not supposed to be here."

"Well, I am." Jacob continued to move.

"She's only thirty feet to your south," Toby said. "Don't make me regret keeping you in the loop."

"I've got her in my sights," Jacob whispered. Now, all he had to do was make sure he didn't spook her. He stopped, hiding behind a tree. He glanced around, finding five different agents or cops. He signaled to one of them, who pointed for him to circle back toward Edward.

Katie was only twenty feet from Edward. She continued heading southwest at a brisk jog, weaving between trees.

Jacob made his way around in front of her as fast as he could. He dodged behind a tree and stuck his head out, putting his finger in front of his lips.

Her eyes went wide, and she slowed.

Keep running, he mouthed.

She continued through the woods as if she'd never

seen him while he ducked his head back behind the tree.

He couldn't risk being seen by Edward. At least, not yet.

Jacob twisted his body, peeking from the other side of the tree. Edward had inched forward a few feet, obviously keeping Katie in his sights.

They needed a little more space between him and Katie before he intervened. Jacob glanced toward the agent hiding to the right of Edward.

The agent nodded.

Jacob stepped from out of his hiding place only ten paces in front of Edward.

"What the fuck are you doing here?" Edward held his bow at the ready.

"It looked like a nice day for a hike." Jacob raised his weapon.

"Tsk, tsk," Edward said. "First, I'd drop that gun if I were you."

"That's not going to happen."

"That's too bad." Edward pulled back on the bowstring. "I didn't want to have to kill a law enforcement man. I really do have a lot of respect for you."

"That's funny."

"I don't see why. My father was a cop. And a good one."

"Then I'm sure he'd be very disappointed in what you've become." Jacob swallowed as two agents stepped in from behind Edward. The goal was always to take a suspect in alive.

But Jacob wouldn't care if Edward ended up face down in the dirt.

"You don't know shit about my family." Edward closed one eye. "And my prey is getting away, so time to put an end to this." He pulled his arm all the way back, bending his elbow.

Fuck.

"Don't do it," Jacob said, just as one of the agents lunged.

But it was too late.

Edward released the arrow.

Jacob jumped to the left, but the arrow still hit his right biceps.

"Jacob," Katie called as he hit the ground. "I'm fine," he ground out as he grabbed his arm, but Katie stopped him. It stung like a motherfucker.

"That asshole shot you." She took off her shirt and wrapped it around his arm.

"It barely touched me." He glanced at his bloody hand. "Okay, maybe it's a little worse than that." A sharp pain crawled from his elbow to his shoulder. He glanced down and saw that the arrow was still lodged in his arm. "Shit. That might not be good." He glanced from his wound to his girlfriend, who only wore a pair of jeans and a sports bra. "You shouldn't have taken off your clothing."

"Do you think I'm going to let you bleed to death?"

"I don't like my buddies seeing you in that."

She laughed. "My bikini shows more skin."

"We'll have to talk about that." He blinked, trying to ignore the pain, but it became impossible. He eased back onto his ass and leaned against a big tree.

Another agent was at his side, tending to his wound.

"I'll be right back," Katie said.

"Where are you going?" he asked.

"To make Edward feel a little pain for shooting the man I love."

Katie leaned over and gave Jacob a quick kiss.

"Katie, he's not worth it," Jacob whispered.

"But you are." She stood and turned.

An agent had hoisted Edward to his feet and cuffed him. She knew his reign of terror was over, but she had a few things she wanted to get off her chest.

Now.

"If you think I'm going to jail, little girl, you've got another thing coming," Edward said with a sinister smile. "You might think your boyfriend and his little friends got me up shit creek without a paddle, but they don't. You wait and see. I'll be out in no time." He leaned forward. "And then you and your dear old dad will need to have a heart to heart."

"Like I said, biology doesn't make someone a father." She stood only inches from Edward and rose on tiptoe. "You are not my dad." She poked him dead center in his chest. "And make no mistake, I'm going to make sure you rot in a prison cell until the day you die if it takes until my last breath."

"Is that a promise, or a threat?"

"Neither. It's a fact." She took a step back. "Get this piece of shit out of here."

"Gladly," one of the agents said.

Jackson came into view, and that's when all her emotions smacked her right in the heart. She glanced over her shoulder, and tears formed in her eyes.

"An ambulance is on the way." Jackson put his arm around her and led her back toward Jacob. "He's going to be fine, you know."

She nodded. "How did you find me?"

"Tracking device in the evidence box that Cameron had put there, in hopes Edward might show up," Jackson said.

"I take it Jacob didn't know about that." Katie took in a deep breath and then let it out slowly.

"If he had, do you think he would have let you go in there like that?"

She let out a short laugh. "Probably not." She knelt next to Jacob. "How are you holding up?"

Jacob blinked. "I'll be better when someone gets that fucking thing out of my arm and pumps me full of morphine."

"Help is ten minutes away," Jackson said.

"Sorry it took so long to get everyone in place." Toby tied off Katie's shirt around the arrow stuck in Jacob's arm. "We had to make sure all the innocents were out of the area, and the spot was secure."

"I know the drill." Jacob dropped his head back. "I'm so looking forward to getting my old job back."

"So, you decided to go back to the DA's office and not to work with your dad?" Katie took his hand and squeezed it.

"I can't defend criminals. I don't care that they deserve a fair trial. I just can't stomach it," Jacob said. "Shit, this hurts."

"Only a few minutes out," Toby said. "Hang tight."

Jacob nodded, catching Katie's gaze. "I did say I'd take a bullet for you once."

"That's not a bullet, so there's still time," Katie said.

Jacob laughed, then coughed. "Semantics."

"Words matter." She cupped his cheek, pressing her lips against his. "And I hope you will always remember these three little words." She smiled. "I love you."

"I love you more."

13

THREE WEEKS LATER...

Katie stood in the front yard of Raif and Isabelle's home, staring at her house across the bay. She couldn't believe that much of the money that had been stolen from the foundation would be returned, as well as some of her personal assets.

She'd be able to restore the Bateman estate to its original beauty, and according to Stacey's husband and father, it would only take a year to do it.

Of course, the foundation would take years to rebuild, but Raif and Isabelle had promised to help, as did many others from the community.

She glanced down at her hand and the engagement ring on her finger. She'd put it on and took it off three times this past week. All three times, it had been when Jacob was out. She loved Jacob. There was no doubt in her mind about that. And she wanted to spend the rest of her life with him.

Another thing she didn't question.

She wasn't sure why she was holding back. Maybe it had to do with the few unknowns left regarding Grace.

"Katie, they're back," Isabelle called.

So much had changed in Katie's world over the last few weeks. So many things that she'd thought had been the truth had turned out to be falsehoods or downright lies. She'd idolized a woman, who while she'd been a victim, still couldn't come to terms with what a monster her husband had truly been.

Or that's what Katie feared.

Grace had said that she'd left Edward because of the lies and the murders, but at the same time, she refused to turn him in and struggled to agree to testify against him. That was what today was all about.

It was Grace's inability to commit one way or the other that'd kept Katie from going to the courthouse. Owen begged her to show a little sympathy and support, but Katie needed her mother to make the right decision on her own and not to be influenced by what Katie wanted, especially if they were ever going to have a relationship moving forward.

Isabelle greeted her by the kitchen sliders. "We might as well wait for them out here." She held a bottle of wine. "I'm hoping it's good news."

"I don't think it'll be good news regardless of how

the judge rules." Katie rubbed her temples as she took a seat around the fire pit. She gladly took the glass of wine that Isabelle offered. The last two weeks had been crazy between Edward refusing to cooperate, which meant he'd go on trial, and it would be the trial of the century.

The funniest part of the entire thing was that Edward kept trying to get Raif to agree to take his case.

That was never going to happen. As of this moment, the case was in the hands of a public defender who was begging Edward to take a plea. No one wanted to argue any kind of defense because there was none. Not with the kind of evidence they had collected.

Although, he was still claiming his innocence.

However, Owen had been exonerated of his sister's murder, and the state of New York had to apologize for wrongful incarceration.

Owen took it in stride and told Katie he'd do it all again if it meant she'd be safe.

She wasn't sure how to take that juicy piece of information. On the one hand, she was grateful to him for caring that much about her. But on the other, he'd lost his entire life. And for what? Katie wasn't sure it wouldn't have been the same outcome had Owen not taken the fall. But what was done was done. Katie couldn't go back and change the past. She could only move forward.

Raif and Jacob stepped through the sliding glass doors.

Jacob still had to keep his arm in a sling, but there had been no major damage, thank goodness.

"Where's Owen?" Isabelle asked.

"He's not far behind," Raif said. "He wanted to give us a little time."

"That wasn't necessary," Isabelle said. "So, what happened?"

"Let us get some wine." Raif took the bottle and poured himself and Jacob a hearty glass. "It was a long day."

Jacob bent over and kissed Katie, good and hard.

She reached up and cupped the back of his neck, massaging gently. "Well, hello," she whispered.

"When I asked for a drink, that wasn't an invitation for the two of you to make out," Raif said.

"I can't help myself." Jacob smiled as he made himself comfortable. He took a big sip of the red liquid. "My girlfriend is irresistible."

"Aw, that's so sweet." Isabelle raised her glass. "It warms my heart to see the two of you back together."

"You and me both, Mom."

"Now that everyone has something to sip on, and we're all seated around the fire, is anyone going to tell us the fate of Katie's mom?" Isabelle asked.

Katie closed her eyes. She wasn't sure she wanted to hear this.

Jacob wrapped his good arm around her shoulders, drawing her close to his body. He pressed his lips on her forehead. "She agreed to testify against him."

"Oh, thank God." Katie blinked open her eyes.

"The FBI will be placing her in protective custody until after the trial, and as long as she continues to cooperate, all charges of obstruction and any other crimes she might have committed will be overlooked," Raif said. "I will continue to be her lawyer—free of charge, of course."

"I can't thank you enough for doing that." Katie let out a long breath.

"It's my pleasure," Raif said. "She's not the same woman I used to know, but she's still a victim."

Katie nodded. It would take a long time before she could fully forgive her mom, but this was a start. "Can I see her?"

"I can make that happen." Jacob lifted his arm and leaned forward, raising his drink. "Maybe even tomorrow."

"I know I should have gone with you, but I just couldn't." Katie stretched out her left hand and found her wine glass.

"Oh, my." Isabelle gasped. "That's my mother's engagement ring."

"Well, I'll be damned." Raif slapped his leg. "When did the two of you make that happen?"

Jacob grabbed her hand and glanced between the ring on her finger and her eyes. "I didn't know you were putting that on?"

"Wait. What?" Isabelle asked. "You didn't propose?"

Katie's cheeks flushed.

"Not exactly," Jacob said. "I told her when she was ready to just put it on." He cocked his head. "Are you saying you're ready?"

Tears filled her eyes. Not much had made sense in the last few weeks, much less years, but this felt perfect. Being with Jacob was easy. Loving him came naturally. And wearing the ring was like wearing her own skin.

"Yes," she said. "I want to get married."

"Mom. Dad. You might want to turn your heads. I'm going to make out with my fiancée."

EPILOGUE

HALLOWEEN...

*O*nly Katie would want to get married on Halloween.

And only the best husband in the world would agree.

Jacob took Katie's chin with his thumb and forefinger. "I love you," he whispered.

"You'd better. Because now you're stuck with me." She smiled, trying not to cry again, but it proved to be impossible.

"Wow. You're doing it again."

"I can't help it. They are happy tears." Typically, crying wasn't something she regularly did, but her hormones had gotten the best of her. Now, all she had to do was find the right words to tell her new husband that he hadn't just gained a wife, but that he was going to have a baby in about seven months, too.

"We got lucky with the weather." He laced his

fingers through hers and tugged her across the yard and onto the front deck.

Shit. Okay, maybe it wasn't going to be right at this moment since she didn't want to do it in a room full of people.

She stepped inside. The Bateman estate was far from completed, but enough had been done to hold a wedding in the front yard, and a small reception in the house.

Thankfully, the normally chilly fall days in upstate New York had decided to be unseasonably warm, and the temperatures were well above fifty. Though, as the sun dropped, so did the warmth wane.

It had been a small ceremony, just family and a few close friends. "Your mom looks a little lost. Have you had a chance to talk to her?"

"No," Katie admitted. "But I should go spend some time with her. I've been avoiding this for so long." She'd only seen her four times since Edward had been arrested and subsequently sentenced to life without the possibility of parole. Theirs was a strained relationship, and while Katie was trying, she had some underlying abandonment issues that she was working through in therapy.

Something that she wanted Grace to join her for. But she had yet to ask, fearing that Grace would say no.

"You don't have to do this on our wedding day, you know."

She glanced into her husband's loving eyes. She and

Jacob had been through so much together. He'd been her rock, and she knew he'd do anything for her. All she had to do was ask. "If I don't do it now, I'll just keep putting it off."

"All right. I'll be right over there with Jackson if you need me."

She kissed her husband before taking a few deep breaths. She made her way across the room. "Hey, Mom," she said.

"Oh. Hi," her mother said. "I'm not used to you calling me that."

"Well, you are my mother."

With a shaky hand, her mom reached out and palmed her cheek. "Thank you for including me. You and Jacob look so happy together."

"We are." Katie leaned into her mom's hand and blinked. "I couldn't get married without you here. Not after everything we've been through."

"I know I've made a lot of mistakes, and I can't change what I've done. I just want you to know that I regret so much, but I'm so grateful that Edward didn't bring you with us. That wouldn't have been any kind of life for you."

"I wish he hadn't taken you." Katie curled her fingers around her mother's wrist. "And you were taken. You might have thought you had a choice, but you didn't. You were a victim."

Her mother nodded slightly. "I'm trying to believe that. Owen keeps telling me that."

Katie shook her head. "I still can't believe he gladly went to prison to save me."

"That's who Owen has always been," her mother said. "He was constantly taking the blame for me when we were kids, and I know he'd do it all over again." Her mother dropped her hand to her side. "I, however, wish I could have done so many things differently."

"Don't beat yourself up, Mom," Katie said. "While I'm sad for what you and Owen had to go through, and for what I had to endure the last couple of years, please know that I had a good childhood. And, in some ways, I wouldn't want to change things, either. Which brings me to a question I have for you."

"What's that?"

"I was hoping you might come to some therapy sessions with me."

"Oh." Her mother squared her shoulders. "I was going to ask you to come with me."

Katie smiled. "I'd love to."

Her mother pulled her in for a big hug. "I never stopped loving you, Katie. Never."

"I know." And now the tears were really flowing. Katie sniffled. This crying shit was for the birds. She took a step back and found a tissue. "Sorry."

"It's your wedding day. It's okay to cry."

"That's what everyone keeps telling me." Katie dabbed at her eyes.

"Is there something wrong?" her mother asked.

Katie shook her head. "I'm just being emotional, and I'm not used to that."

"The only time I was ever like that to the point where I couldn't control it was when I was carrying you, and—oh, my. Are you preg—?"

"Shhh. I haven't told anyone yet. And I think Jacob should be the first to know."

"First to know what?" Jacob looped his arm around her shoulders.

Her mother smiled widely. "That is my cue to get a drink."

Katie took in a deep breath. "Do you like the name Isabelle Grace?"

"It's a nice name," Jacob said with a narrow-eyed stare.

"What about Jonathon Jacob?"

He cocked his head and took a step back. "Why are you combining my brother's name with mine?"

"Because you're going to be a daddy, and we're going to need a name for our kid." She patted the center of his chest.

"Um. What?" Jacob blinked a few times. "Did you just say I'm going to be a father?"

"You two are expecting?" Isabelle practically screamed just as the music stopped playing. "I'm going to be a grandmother?"

The room went dead silent.

"I think I need to sit down." Jacob took Katie by the

hand as he sat on the sofa, pulling her onto his lap. "Are you sure?"

"I am. I didn't plan on telling you this way. It just kind of happened."

"I did wonder why you passed on champagne and wine."

She shrugged. "Not good for the baby."

He placed his hand over her stomach. "A baby. We're really having a baby?"

She nodded.

He palmed her cheek. "I love you, Katie."

"I love you more."

Thank you for taking the time to read *Legacy of Lies*.
Please feel free to leave an honest review.
If you haven't read *Dark Legacy*, you can download your copy today! *Secret Legacy* can pre-order now!

ABOUT THE AUTHOR

Jen Talty is the *USA Today* Bestselling Author of Contemporary Romance, Romantic Suspense, and Paranormal Romance. In the fall of 2020, her short story was selected and featured in a 1001 Dark Nights Anthology. She is currently contracted to write in the With Me in Seattle series by Kristen Proby with Lady Boss Press, as well as Susan Stoker's Special Forces: Operation Alpha and Elle James's Brotherhood Protectors.

Regardless of the genre, her goal is to take you on a ride that will leave you floating under the sun with warmth in your heart. She writes stories about broken heroes and heroines who aren't necessarily looking for romance, but in the end, they find the kind of love books are written about :).

She first started writing while carting her kids to one hockey rink after the other, averaging 170 games per year between 3 kids in 2 countries and 5 states. Her first book, IN TWO WEEKS was originally published in 2007. In 2010 she helped form a publishing company (Cool Gus Publishing) with *NY Times* Bestselling Author Bob Mayer where she ran the technical side of the business through 2016.

Jen is currently enjoying the next phase of her life…the empty nester! She and her husband reside in Jupiter, Florida.

Grab a glass of vino, kick back, relax, and let the romance roll in…

Sign up for my Newsletter (https://dl.bookfunnel.com/82gm8b9k4y) where I often give away free books before publication.

Join my private Facebook group (https://www.facebook.com/groups/191706547909047/) where I post exclusive excerpts and discuss all things murder and love!

And on Bookbub: bookbub.com/authors/jen-talty

- facebook.com/AuthorJenTalty
- instagram.com/jen_talty
- bookbub.com/authors/jen-talty
- amazon.com/author/jentalty
- pinterest.com/jentalty

ALSO BY JEN TALTY

Club Temptation
SWEET TEMPTATION

Legacy Series
Dark Legacy
Legacy of Lies
Secret Legacy

With Me In Seattle
INVESTIGATE WITH ME
SAIL WITH ME
FLY WITH ME

The Monroes
COLOR ME YOURS
COLOR ME SMART
COLOR ME FREE
COLOR ME LUCKY
COLOR ME ICE

It's all in the Whiskey
JOHNNIE WALKER

GEORGIA MOON

JACK DANIELS

JIM BEAM

WHISKEY SOUR

WHISKEY COBBLER

WHISKEY SMASH

Search and Rescue

PROTECTING AINSLEY

PROTECTING CLOVER

PROTECTING OLYMPIA

PROTECTING FREEDOM

PROTECTING PRINCESS

NY STATE TROOPER SERIES

In Two Weeks

Dark Water

Deadly Secrets

Murder in paradise Bay

To Protect His own

Deadly Seduction

When A Stranger Calls

His Deadly Past

The Corkscrew Killer

Brand New Novella for the First Responders series
A spin off from the NY State Troopers series
PLAYING WITH FIRE
PRIVATE CONVERSATION
THE RIGHT GROOM
AFTER THE FIRE
CAUGHT IN THE FLAMES

The Men of Thief Lake
REKINDLED
DESTINY'S DREAM

Federal Investigators
JANE DOE'S RETURN
THE BUTTERFLY MURDERS

The Aegis Network
THE LIGHTHOUSE
HER LAST HOPE
THE LAST FLIGHT
THE RETURN HOME
THE MATRIARCH

The Collective Order
THE LOST SISTER
THE LOST SOLDIER

THE LOST SOUL
THE LOST CONNECTION
A Spin-Off Series: Witches Academy Series
THE NEW ORDER

Special Forces Operation Alpha
BURNING DESIRE
BURNING KISS
BURNING SKIES
BURNING LIES
BURNING HEART
BURNING BED
REMEMBER ME ALWAYS

The Brotherhood Protectors
Out of the Wild
ROUGH JUSTICE
ROUGH AROUND THE EDGES
ROUGH RIDE
ROUGH EDGE
ROUGH BEAUTY

The Brotherhood Protectors
The Saving Series
SAVING LOVE

SAVING MAGNOLIA
SAVING LEATHER

Hot Hunks
Cove's Blind Date Blows Up
My Everyday Hero – Ledger
Tempting Tavor

Holiday Romances
A CHRISTMAS GETAWAY
<u>ALASKAN CHRISTMAS</u>
WHISPERS
CHRISTMAS IN THE SAND
CHRISTMAS IN JULY

Heroes & Heroines on the Field
TAKING A RISK
TEE TIME

The Twilight Crossing Series
THE BLIND DATE
SPRING FLING
SUMMER'S GONE
WINTER WEDDING

Witches and Werewolves

LADY SASS

ALL THAT SASS

www.ingramcontent.com/pod-product-compliance
Lightning Source LLC
Chambersburg PA
CBHW072337130725
29542CB00010BA/560